The Hour of the Star

CLARICE LISPECTOR

The Hour of the Star

TRANSLATED WITH AN AFTERWORD BY
GIOVANNI PONTIERO

A NEW DIRECTIONS BOOK

This translation was originally published in Great Britain in 1986
by Carcanet Press Limited.
First published as New Directions Paperbook 733 in 1992
Published simultaneously in Canada by Penguin Books Canada Limited
Manufactured in the United States of America.
New Directions Books are printed on acid-free paper.

Library of Congress Cataloging-in-Publication Data
Lispector, Clarice.
    [Hora da estrela. English]
    The hour of the star / Clarice Lispector ; translated with an
afterword by Giovanni Pontiero.
        p.   cm. —(New Directions paperbook ; 733)
    Translation of: A hora da estrela.
    ISBN 0-8112-1190-8 (acid-free) : $8.95
    I. Title.
PQ9697.L585H6713   1992
869.3—dc20   91-29995
                                                                  CIP

New Directions Books are published for James Laughlin
by New Directions Publishing Corporation,
80 Eighth Avenue, New York 10011

For Olga Borelli

Clarice stirs in the greater depths,
where the word finds its true meaning,
portraying mankind.

('Vision of Clarice Lispector')
Carlos Drummond de Andrade

The Author's Dedication
(alias Clarice Lispector)

I DEDICATE this narrative to dear old Schumann and his beloved Clara who are now, alas, nothing but dust and ashes. I dedicate it to the deep crimson of my blood as someone in his prime. I dedicate it, above all, to those gnomes, dwarfs, sylphs, and nymphs who inhabit my life. I dedicate it to the memory of my years of hardship when everything was more austere and honourable, and I had never eaten lobster. I dedicate it to the tempest of Beethoven. To the vibrations of Bach's neutral colours. To Chopin who leaves me weak. To Stravinsky who terrifies me and makes me soar in flames. To *Death and Transfiguration*, in which Richard Strauss predicts my fate. Most of all, I dedicate it to the day's vigil and to day itself, to the transparent voice of

Debussy, to Marlos Nobre, to Prokofiev, to Carl Orff and Schoenberg, to the twelve-tone composers, to the strident notes of an electronic generation — to all those musicians who have touched within me the most alarming and unsuspected regions; to all those prophets of our age who have revealed me to myself and made me explode into: me. This me that is you, for I cannot bear to be simply me, I need others in order to stand up, giddy and awkward as I am, for what can one do except meditate in order to plunge into that total void which can only be attained through meditation. Meditation need not bear fruit: meditation can be an end in itself. I meditate without words or themes. What troubles my existence is writing.

And we must never forget that if the atom's structure is invisible, it is none the less real. I am aware of the existence of many things I have never seen. And you too. One cannot prove the existence of what is most real but the essential thing is to believe. To weep and believe. This story unfolds in a state of emergency and public calamity. It is an unfinished book because it offers no answer. An answer I hope someone somewhere in the world may be able to provide. You perhaps? It is a story in technicolour to add a touch of luxury, for heaven knows, I need that too. Amen for all of us.

THE HOUR
OF THE STAR

The Blame is Mine
or
The Hour of the Star
or
Let Her Fend for Herself
or
The Right to Protest

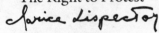

.As for the Future.
or
Singing the Blues
or
She Doesn't Know How to Protest
or
A Sense of Loss
or
Whistling in the Dark Wind
or
I Can Do Nothing
or
A Record of Preceding Events
or
A Tearful Tale
or
A Discreet Exit by the Back Door

EVERYTHING in the world began with a yes. One molecule said yes to another molecule and life was born. But before prehistory there was the prehistory of prehistory and there was the never and there was the yes. It was ever so. I do not know why, but I do know that the universe never began.

Let no one be mistaken. I only achieve simplicity with enormous effort.

So long as I have questions to which there are no answers, I shall go on writing. How does one start at the beginning, if things happen before they actually happen? If before the pre-prehistory there already existed apocalyptic monsters? If this history does not exist, it will come to exist. To think is an act. To feel is a fact. Put the two together — it is me who is writing what I am writing. God is the world. The truth is always some inner power without explanation. The more genuine part of my life is unrecognizable, extremely intimate and impossible to define. My heart has shed every desire and reduced itself to one final or initial beat. The toothache that passes through this narrative has given me a sharp twinge right in the mouth. I break out into a strident, high-pitched, syncopated melody. It is the sound of my own pain, of someone who carries this world where there is so little happiness. Happiness? I have never come across a more foolish word, invented by all those unfortunate girls from north-eastern Brazil.

I should explain that this story will emerge from a gradual vision — for the past two and a half years I have slowly started discovering the whys and the wherefores. It is the vision of the imminence of . . . of what? Perhaps I shall find out later. Just as I am writing at the same time as I am being read. Only I do not start with the ending that would justify the beginning — as death appears to comment on life — because I must record the preceding events.

Even as I write this I feel ashamed at pouncing on you with a narrative that is so open and explicit. A narrative, however, from which blood surging with life might flow only to coagulate into lumps of trembling jelly. Will this story become my own coagulation one day? Who can tell? If there is any truth in it — and clearly the story is true even though invented — let everyone see it reflected in himself for we are all one and the same person, and he who is not poor in terms of money is poor in spirit or feeling for he lacks something more precious than gold — for there are those who do not possess that essential essence.

How do I know all that is about to follow if it is unfamiliar and something I have never experienced? In a street in Rio de Janeiro I caught a glimpse of perdition on the face of a girl from the North-east. Without mentioning that I myself was

12

raised as a child in the North-east. Besides, I know about certain things simply by living. Anyone who lives, knows, even without knowing that he or she knows. So, dear readers, you know more than you imagine, however much you may deny it.

I do not intend to write anything complicated, although I am obliged to use the words that sustain you. The story — I have decided with an illusion of free will — should have some seven characters, and obviously I am one of the more important.

I, Rodrigo S.M. A traditional tale for I have no desire to be modish and invent colloquialisms under the guise of originality. So I shall attempt, contrary to my normal method, to write a story with a beginning, a middle, and a 'grand finale' followed by silence and falling rain.

A story that is patently open and explicit yet holds certain secrets — starting with one of the book's titles 'As For The Future', preceded and followed by a full stop. This is no caprice on my part — hopefully this need for confinement will ultimately become clear. (The ending is still so vague yet, were my poverty to permit, I should like it to be grandiose.) If, instead of a full stop, the title were followed by dotted lines, it would remain open to every kind of speculation on your part, however morbid or pitiless. It is true that I, too, feel no pity for my main character, the girl from the North-east: I want my story to be cold and impartial. Unlike the reader, I reserve the right to be devastatingly cold, for this is not simply a narrative, but above all primary life that breathes, breathes, breathes. Made of porous material, I shall one day assume the form of a molecule with its potential explosion of atoms. What I am writing is something more than mere invention; it is my duty to relate everything about this girl among thousands of others like her. It is my duty, however unrewarding, to confront her with her own existence.

For one has a right to shout.

So, I am shouting.

A simple shout that begs no charity. I know that there are girls who sell their bodies, their only real possession, in exchange for a good dinner rather than the usual mortadella sandwich. But the person whom I am about to describe scarcely has a body to sell; nobody desires her, she is a harmless virgin whom nobody needs. It strikes me that I don't need her either and that what I am writing could be written by another. Another writer, of course, but it would have to be a man for a woman would weep her heart out.

There are thousands of girls like this girl from the Northeast to be found in the slums of Rio de Janeiro, living in bedsitters or toiling behind counters for all they are worth. They aren't even aware of the fact that they are superfluous and that nobody cares a damn about their existence. Few of them ever complain and as far as I know they never protest, for there is no one to listen.

I am warming up before making a start, rubbing my hands together to summon up my courage. I can remember a time when I used to pray in order to kindle my spirit: movement is spirit. Prayer was a means of confronting myself in silence away from the gaze of others. As I prayed I emptied my soul — and this emptiness is everything that I can ever hope to possess. Apart from this, there is nothing. But emptiness, too, has its value and somehow resembles abundance. One way of obtaining is not to search, one way of possessing is not to ask; simply to believe that my inner silence is the solution to my — to my mystery.

It is my intention, as I suggested earlier, to write with ever greater simplicity. Besides, the material at my disposal is all too sparse and mundane, I possess few details about my characters and those details are not very revealing; details that laboriously stem from me only to return to me; the craft of carpentry.

Remember that, no matter what I write, my basic material is the word. So this story will consist of words that form phrases from which there emanates a secret meaning that exceeds both words and phrases. Like every writer, I am clearly tempted to use succulent terms: I have at my command magnificent adjectives, robust nouns, and verbs so agile that they glide through the atmosphere as they move into action. For surely words are actions? Yet I have no intention of adorning the word, for were I to touch the girl's bread, that bread would turn to gold — and the girl (she is nineteen years old) the girl would be unable to bite into it, and consequently die of hunger. So I must express myself simply in order to capture her delicate and shadowy existence. With humility I confine myself — without making too much fuss about my humility for then it would no longer be humility — I confine myself to narrating the unremarkable adventures of a girl living in a hostile city. A girl who should have stayed in the backwoods of Alagoas wearing a cotton dress and avoiding the typewriter, for she was barely literate and had only received three years of primary schooling. She was so backward that when she typed she was obliged to copy out every word slowly, letter by letter. Her aunt had given her a crash course in typing. As a result, the girl had acquired some dignity: she was a typist at last, even though she appeared to have some difficulty in stringing two consonants together. When she copied out the attractive, rotund handwriting of the boss, whom she idolized, the word 'designate' became 'desiginate', for that is how she herself would have pronounced it.

Forgive me if I add something more about myself since my identity is not very clear, and when I write I am surprised to find that I possess a destiny. Who has not asked himself at some time or other: am I a monster or is this what it means to be a person?

First of all, I must make it clear that this girl does not know herself apart from the fact that she goes on living aimlessly. Were she foolish enough to ask herself 'Who am I?', she would fall flat on her face. For the question 'Who am

I?' creates a need. And how does one satisfy that need? To probe oneself is to recognize that one is incomplete.

The person of whom I am about to speak is so simple-minded that she often smiles at other people on the street. No one acknowledges her smile for they don't even notice her.

Coming back to myself: what I am about to write cannot be assimilated by minds that expect much and crave sophistication. For what I am about to express will be quite stark. Although it may have as its background — even now — the tormented shadows that haunt my dreams as I sleep tormented at night. Do not, therefore, expect stars in what follows for nothing will scintillate. This is opaque material and by its very nature it is despised by everyone. This story has no melody that could be rightly termed *cantabile*. Its rhythm is frequently discordant. It also contains facts. I have always been enthusiastic about facts without literature — facts are hard stones and I am much more interested in action than in meditation. There is no way of escaping facts.

I ask myself if I should jump ahead in time and sketch out an ending immediately. As it happens, I have no idea how this story will end. I also realize that I must proceed step by step in accordance with a period of time measured in hours: even animals struggle with time. This, too, is my first condition; to proceed slowly notwithstanding my impatience to tell you about this girl.

In writing this story, I shall yield to emotion and I know perfectly well that every day is one more day stolen from death. In no sense an intellectual, I write with my body. And what I write is like a dank haze. The words are sounds transfused with shadows that intersect unevenly, stalactites, woven lace, transposed organ music. I can scarcely invoke the words to describe this pattern, vibrant and rich, morbid and obscure, its counterpoint the deep bass of sorrow. *Allegro con brio.* I shall attempt to extract gold from charcoal. I know that I am holding up the narrative and playing at ball

16

without a ball. Is the fact an act? I swear that this book is composed without words: like a mute photograph. This book is a silence: an interrogation.

I suspect that this lengthy preamble is intended to conceal the poverty of my story, for I am apprehensive. Before this typist entered my life, I was a reasonably contented chap despite my limited success as a writer. Things were somehow so good that they were in danger of becoming very bad because what is fully mature is very close to rotting.

But the idea of transcending my own limits suddenly appealed to me. This happened when I decided to write about reality, since reality exceeds me. Whatever one understands by reality. Will what I am about to narrate sound mushy? It has that tendency but I am determined to sound dry and severe. At least what I am writing begs no favours or assistance from anyone: so-called sorrow is borne with the dignity of an aristocrat.

It seems that I am changing my style of writing. Not being a professional writer, I please myself what I write about — and I must write about this girl from the North-east otherwise I shall choke. She points an accusing finger and I can only defend myself by writing about her. I tend to write with bold, severe strokes like a painter. I shall struggle with facts as if they were those impossible stones which I mentioned earlier. How I should love to hear the pealing of bells in order to work up some enthusiasm as I decipher reality: to see angels flutter like transparent wasps around my fevered head, this head that longs to be ultimately transformed into an object-thing, because so much more simple.

Is it possible that actions exceed words? As I write — let things be known by their real names. Each thing is a word. And when there is no word, it must be invented. This God of yours who commanded us to invent.

Why do I write? First of all because I have captured the spirit of the language and at times it is the form that constitutes the content. I write, therefore, not for the girl from the North-east but for the much more serious reason of *force majeure*, or as they say in formal petitions by 'force of law'.

My strength undoubtedly resides in solitude. I am not afraid of tempestuous storms or violent gales for I am also the night's darkness. Even though I cannot bear to hear whistling or footsteps in the dark. Darkness? It reminds me of a former girl friend. She was sexually experienced and there was such darkness inside her body. I have never forgotten her: one never forgets a person with whom one has slept. The event remains branded on one's living flesh like a tattoo and all who witness the stigma take flight in horror.

I now want to speak of the girl from the North-east. It's as follows: like some vagrant bitch she was guided entirely by her own remote control. For she had reduced herself to herself. After successive failures, I have also reduced myself, but I still want to discover the world and its God.

I should like to add some details about the young girl and myself; we live exclusively in the present because forever and eternally it is the day of today, and the day of tomorrow will be a today. Eternity is the state of things at this very moment.

See how apprehensive I have become since putting down words about the girl from the North-east. The question is: how do I write? I can verify that I write by ear, just as I learned English and French by ear. My antecedents as a writer? I am a man who possesses more money than those who go hungry, and this makes me in some ways dishonest. I only lie at the precise hour of lying. But when I write I do not lie. What else? Yes, I belong to no social category, marginal as I am. The upper classes consider me a strange creature, the middle classes regard me with suspicion, afraid that I might unsettle them, while the lower classes avoid me.

18

No, it is not easy to write. It is as hard as breaking rocks. Sparks and splinters fly like shattered steel.

I am scared of starting. I do not even know the girl's name. It goes without saying that this story drives me to despair because it is too straightforward. What I propose to narrate sounds easy and within everyone's grasp. But its elaboration is extremely difficult. I must render clear something that is almost obliterated and can scarcely be deciphered. With stiff, contaminated fingers I must touch the invisible in its own squalor.

Of one thing I am certain: this narrative will combine with something delicate: the creation of an entire human being who is as much alive as I am. I have taken care of her because my mandate is simply to reveal her presence so that you may recognize her on the street, moving ever so cautiously because of her quivering frailty. And should my narrative turn out to be sad? Later, I shall amost certainly write something more cheerful, but why cheerful? Because I, too, am a man of hosannas and perhaps one day I shall intone praises instead of the misfortunes of the girl from the North-east.

Meantime, I want to walk naked or in rags; I want to experience at least once the insipid flavour of the Host. To eat communion bread will be to taste the world's indifference, and to immerse myself in nothingness. This will be my courage: to abandon comforting sentiments from the past.

There is little comfort now. In order to speak about the girl I mustn't shave for days. I must acquire dark circles under my eyes from lack of sleep: dozing from sheer exhaustion like a manual labourer. Also wearing threadbare clothes. I am doing all this to put myself on the same footing as the girl from the North-east. Fully aware that I might have to present myself in a more convincing manner to societies who demand a great deal from someone who is typing at this very moment.

Yes, all this, for history is history. But knowing beforehand so as never to forget that the word is the fruit of the word. The word must resemble the word. To attain the word is my first duty to myself. The word must not be adorned and become aesthetically worthless; it must be simply itself. It is also true that I have attempted to acquire a certain refinement of feeling and that this extreme refinement should not break into a perpetual line. At the same time, I have attempted to imitate the deep, raw, dense sound of the trombone, for no good reason except that I feel so nervous about writing that I might explode into a fit of uncontrollable laughter. I want to accept my freedom without reaching the conclusion like so many others: that existence is only for fools and lunatics: for it would seem that to exist is illogical.

The action of this story will result in my transfiguration into someone else and in my ultimate materialization into an object. Perhaps I might even acquire the sweet tones of the flute and become entwined in a creeper vine.

But let us return to today. As is known, today is today. No one understands my meaning and I can obscurely hear mocking laughter with that rapid, edgy cackling of old men. I also hear measured footsteps in the road. I tremble with fear. Just as well that what I am about to write is already written deep inside me. I must reproduce myself with the delicacy of a white butterfly. This idea of the white butterfly stems from the feeling that, should the girl marry, she will marry looking as slender and ethereal as any virgin dressed in white. Perhaps she will not marry? To be frank, I am holding her destiny in my hands and yet I am powerless to invent with any freedom: I follow a secret, fatal line. I am forced to seek a truth that transcends me. Why should I write about a young girl whose poverty is so evident? Perhaps because within her there is seclusion. Also because in her poverty of body and soul one touches sanctity and I long to feel the breath of life hereafter. In order to become greater than I am, for I am so little. I write because I have nothing better to do in this world: I am superfluous and last in the world of men. I write because I am desperate and weary. I can no longer bear the routine of my existence and, were it not for the constant novelty of writing, I should die symbolically each day. Yet I am prepared to leave quietly by the back door. I have experienced almost everything, even passion and despair. Now I only wish to possess what might have been but never was.

I seem to know the most intimate details about this girl from the North-east because I live with her. And since I have discovered almost everything about her, she has clung to my skin like some viscous glue or contaminating mud. When I was a child, I read the story of the old man who was afraid to cross the river. Whereupon a youth appeared who also wished to cross to the other side. The old man seized the opportunity and begged him:

— Please take me with you. You can carry me on your back.

The youth agreed and once they were safely across he said to the old man:

— We've arrived. You can get down now.

But the old man, who was very sly and astute, replied:

— Oh no! It's so comfortable up here that I intend to stay put!

The typist doesn't want to get off my back. I now realize that poverty is both ugly and promiscuous. That's why I cannot say whether my narrative will be — will be what? I can reveal nothing for I still haven't worked up enough enthusiasm to write the story. Will there be a plot? Yes, there will. But what plot? That, too, I cannot reveal. I am not trying to cause anguished and voracious expectancy: I simply do not know what awaits me. I have a restless character on my hands who escapes me at every turn and expects me to retrieve her.

I forgot to mention that everything I am now writing is accompanied by the emphatic ruffle of a military drum. The moment I start to tell my story — the noise of the drum will suddenly cease.

I see the girl from the North-east looking in the mirror and — the ruffle of a drum — in the mirror there appears my own face, weary and unshaven. We have reversed roles so completely. Without a shadow of doubt she is a physical person. And what is more: she is a girl who has never seen her naked body because she is much too embarrassed. Embarrassed because she is a prude or because she is ugly? I ask myself how I am going to cope with so many facts without coming to grief. The figurative suddenly appeals to me. I create human action and tremble. Suddenly I crave the figurative like the painter who only uses abstract colours but wants to prove that he does so deliberately and not because he has no talent for drawing. In order to draw the girl, I must control my emotions. In order to capture her soul, I must nourish myself frugally on fruit and drink chilled white wine because it is stifling in this cubby-hole where I have locked myself away and where I feel a sudden urge to see the world. I've also had to give up sex and football. And avoid all human contact. Shall I go back one day to my former way of life? I seriously doubt it. I should also mention that I read nothing these days for fear that I might adulterate the simplicity of my language with useless refinements. For as I explained, the word is my instrument and must resemble the word. Or am I not a writer? More actor than writer, for with only one system of punctuation

22

at my disposal, I juggle with intonation and force another's breathing to accompany my text.

I forgot to mention that the record that is about to begin — for I can no longer bear the onslaught of facts — the record that is about to begin is written under the sponsorship of the most popular soft drink in the world even though it does not earn me anything; a soft drink that is distributed throughout the world. It is the same soft drink that sponsored the recent earthquake in Guatemala. Despite the fact that it tastes of nail polish, toilet soap and chewed plastic. None of this prevents people from loving it with servility and subservience. Also because — and I am now going to say something strange that only I can understand — this drink which contains coca *is today*. It allows people to be modern and to move with the times.

As for the girl, she exists in an impersonal limbo, untouched by what is worst or best. She merely exists, inhaling and exhaling, inhaling and exhaling. Why should there be anything more? Her existence is sparse. Certainly. But why should I feel guilty? Why should I try to relieve myself of the burden of not having done anything concrete to help the girl? This girl — I see that I have almost started telling my story — this girl who slept in cheap cotton underwear with faint but rather suspicious bloodstains. In an effort to fall asleep on cold wintry nights, she would curl up into a ball, receiving and giving out her own scant warmth. She slept with her mouth wide open because of her stuffed-up nostrils, dead to the world from sheer exhaustion.

I must add one important detail to help the reader understand the narrative: it is accompanied from start to finish by the faintest yet nagging twinge of toothache, caused by an exposed nerve. The story will also be accompanied throughout by the plangent tones of a violin played by a musician on the street corner. His face is thin and sallow as if he had just died. Perhaps he is dead. I have explained these details at great length for fear of having promised too much and

23

offering too little. My story is almost trivial. The trick is to begin suddenly, like plunging into an icy sea and bearing its intense coldness with suicidal courage. I am about to begin in the middle by telling you that —

— that she was inept. Inept for living. She had no idea how to cope with life and she was only vaguely aware of her own inner emptiness. Were she capable of explaining herself, she might well confide: the world stands outside me. I stand outside myself. (It's going to be difficult to tell this story. Even though I have nothing to do with the girl, I shall have to write everything through her, trapped as I am by my own fears. The facts are sonorous but among the facts there is a murmuring. It is the murmuring that frightens me.)

The girl had no way of coping. So much so, (bang) that she made no protest when the boss of her firm which distributed pulley equipment bluntly warned her (a bluntness she seemed to provoke with that foolish expression on her face as if begging to be slapped) that he was only prepared to keep on her workmate Glória. He told her he was fed up with her typing mistakes and those blots she invariably made on the paper. The girl felt that she ought to say something to show respect for this boss with whom she was secretly infatuated.

— Please forgive all the trouble I've caused. Senhor Raimundo Silveira, who had already turned his back on her, looked round surprised by the girl's politeness, and something in her docile expression forced him to speak less harshly, and grudgingly concede:

— Well, you needn't leave right away. Let's see how things work out.

After receiving this warning, the girl went to the lavatory where she could be alone, for she felt quite shaken. She examined herself mechanically in the mirror above the filthy hand basin that was badly cracked and full of hairs: the image of her own existence. The dark, tarnished mirror scarcely reflected any image. Perhaps her physical existence

24

had vanished? This illusion soon passed and she saw her entire face distorted by the tarnished mirror; her nose had grown as huge as those false noses made of papier mâché donned by circus clowns. She studied herself and mused: so young and yet so tarnished.

(There are those who have. And there are those who have not. It's very simple: the girl had not. Hadn't what? Simply this: she had not. If you get my meaning that's fine. If you don't, it's still fine. But why am I bothering about this girl when what I really want is wheat that turns ripe and golden in summer?)

When she was a little girl, her aunt, in order to frighten her, insisted that the vampire — the one that sucks human blood by biting its victims in the flesh of the neck — casts no reflection in the mirror. She reckoned that it might not be such a bad thing being a vampire, for the blood would add a touch of pink to her sallow complexion. For she gave the impression of having no blood unless a day might come when she would have to spill it.

The girl had drooping shoulders like those of a darning-woman. She had learned to darn as a child, and she might have made more of her life had she devoted herself to the delicate task of mending, perhaps even with silken threads. Or even more luxurious: shiny satin, a kiss of souls. The darning-needle turned mosquito. A granule of sugar carried on an ant's back. She was as light-headed as an idiot, only she was no idiot. She wasn't even aware that she was unhappy. The one thing she had was faith. In what? In you? It isn't necessary to have faith in anyone or in anything — it is enough to have faith. This often endowed her with a state of grace. For she had never lost faith.

(The girl worries me so much that I feel drained. She has drained me empty. And the less she demands, the more she worries me. I feel frustrated and annoyed. A raging desire to smash dishes and break windows. How can I avenge my-self? Or rather, how can I get satisfaction? I've found the answer: by loving my dog that consumes more food than she does. Why does she not fight back? Has she no pluck? No, she is sweet and docile.)

Her eyes were enormous, round, bulging and inquisitive — she had the expression of someone with a broken wing — some deficiency of the thyroid gland — questioning eyes. Whom was she questioning? God? She did not think about God, nor did God think about her. God belongs to those who succeed in pinning Him down. God appears in a moment of distraction. She asked no questions. She divined that there were no answers. Was she foolish enough to ask? Only to get a blunt *no* in reply? Perhaps she thought about this futile question so that no one could ever accuse her one day of never having asked. Not knowing who to turn to, she appeared to have answered her own question: it is so because it is so. Could there be some other answer? If anyone knows of a better one, let him speak up for I have been waiting for years.

Meanwhile, the clouds are white and the sky is blue. Why is there so much God? At the expense of men.

She had been born with a legacy of misfortune, a creature from nowhere with the expression of someone who apologizes for occupying too much space. Lost in thought, she examined the blotches on her face in the mirror. In Alagoas they had a special name for this condition — it was commonly believed to be caused by the liver. The girl concealed her blotches with a thick layer of white powder which gave the impression that she had been whitewashed but it was preferable to looking sallow. Her general appearance was grimy for she rarely washed. During the day she wore a blouse and skirt, at night she slept in her underwear. Her room-mates didn't have the courage to tell her about her stale body odour. And since she herself seemed to be oblivious of the fact, they were afraid of hurting her feelings. There was nothing irridescent about her, although the parts of her skin unaffected by the blotches had the subtle glow of

26

opals. Not that it mattered. No one paid any attention to her on the street, for she was as appetizing as cold coffee.

And so her days passed. The girl blew her nose on the hem of her petticoat. She lacked that elusive quality known as charm. I am the only person who finds her charming. As the author, I alone love her. I suffer on her account. And I alone may say to her: 'What do you ask of me weeping, that I would not give you singing?' The girl did not know that she existed, just as a dog doesn't know that it's a dog. Therefore she wasn't aware of her own unhappiness. The only thing she desired was to live. She could not explain, for she didn't probe her situation. Perhaps she felt there was some glory in living. She thought that a person was obliged to be happy. So she was happy. Before being born was she an idea? Before being born was she dead? And after being born was she about to die? What a thin slice of water melon.

There are few facts to relate and I am still not sure how this story will develop.

Now (bang) with a few rapid strokes I shall delineate the girl's previous history up to the moment when she stood before the mirror in the lavatory.

She was hopelessly rachitic at birth, the inheritance of the backwoods — the legacy of misfortune I mentioned earlier.

When she was two years old, her parents died of typhoid fever in the backwoods of Alagoas, in that region where the devil is said to have lost his boots. Much later she went to live in Maceió with her maiden aunt, a sanctimonious spinster, and the girl's only surviving relative in the whole wide world. On occasion the girl would recall some incident from her time there. For instance, her aunt rapping her on the head because the old woman believed that the crown of the head was the vital part of one's body. Her aunt would use her knuckles to rap that head of skin and bones which suffered from a calcium deficiency. She would thrash the girl not only because she derived some sensuous pleasure from thrashing her — the old girl found the idea of sexual

27

intercourse so disgusting that she had never married — but also because she considered it her duty to see that the girl did not finish up like many another girl in Maceió standing on street corners with a lit cigarette waiting to pick up a man. So far the girl had shown no signs of becoming a prostitute one day. Even puberty seemed alien to her destiny. Puberty was slow in coming but even among weeds there exists a need for sunlight. The girl soon forgot those thrashings. If you wait patiently, the pain soon passes. But what pained her more was to be denied her favourite dessert: guava preserve with cheese, the only real passion in her life. Her sly old aunt enjoyed punishing her in this way. The girl didn't dare ask why she was always being punished. One doesn't have to know everything and not knowing became an important factor in her life.

Not knowing sounds awful, but it was not so awful for the girl knew lots of things just as a dog knows how to wag its tail or a beggar how to feel hungry: things happen and you suddenly know. No one would teach her how to die one day: yet one day she would surely die as if she had already learned by heart how to play the starring role. For at the hour of death you become a celebrated film star, it is a moment of glory for everyone, when the choral music scales the top notes.

When she was tiny, the girl dearly longed to possess a pet animal. Her aunt, however, decided that an animal in the house would simply mean one more mouth to feed. The girl resigned herself, convinced that she was only fit for breeding fleas and that she didn't deserve a dog's affection. Her aunt's constant reproaches had taught her to keep her head lowered. The old girl's sanctimonious ways, however, had failed to influence her. Once her aunt was dead, the girl never again set foot inside a church. She had no religious feeling and the divinities made no impression.

Life is like that: you press a button and life lights up. Except that the girl didn't know which button to press. She wasn't even aware that she lived in a technological society where she was a mere cog in the machine. One thing, however, did worry her: she no longer knew if she had ever had a father or mother. She had forgotten her origins. If she had thought hard, she might have concluded that she had sprouted from the soil of Alagoas inside a mushroom that soon rotted. She could speak, of course, but had little to say. No sooner do I succeed in persuading her to speak, than she slips through my fingers.

Notwithstanding her aunt's death, the girl was certain that for her things would be different. She would never die. (It's my obsession to become the other man. In this case, the other woman. Pale and feeling weak, I tremble just like her.)

The definable is making me a little weary. I prefer truths that carry no prophecies. When I eventually rid myself of this story, I shall withdraw to the more arbitrary realm of vague prophecies. I did not invent this girl. She forced her being upon me. She was by no means mentally retarded: she was as helpless and trusting as any fool. At least the girl didn't have to beg for food. (There were others who were even more abandoned and starving.) I alone love her.

Then — who knows for what reason — she arrived in Rio, the incredible Rio de Janeiro, where her aunt had found her a job. Then her aunt had died, and the girl was on her own, lodging in a bedsitter with four other girls who worked as shop-assistants at a well-known department store.

The bedsitter was in an old, colonial-style tenement in Acre Street, a red-light district near the docks inhabited by women who picked up seamen in the streets between the depots of charcoal and cement. Those polluted docks made the girl yearn for some future. (What's happening? It's as if I were listening to a lively tune being played on the piano — a sign perhaps that the girl will have a brilliant future? I am consoled by this possibility and will do everything in my power to make it come to pass.)

Acre Street. What a slum. The plump rats of Acre Street. I keep well away from the place. To be frank, I am terrified of that dark hole and its depraved inhabitants.

From time to time, the girl was lucky enough to hear a cockerel welcome the dawn. Then she would remember the backwoods of Alagoas with nostalgia. Where could there be room for a cockerel to crow in that warren of warehouses storing goods for export and import? (If the reader is financially secure and enjoys the comforts of life, he must step out of himself and see how others live. If he is poor, he will not be reading this story because what I have to say is superfluous for anyone who often feels the pangs of hunger. Here I am acting as a safety-valve for you and the tedious bourgeoisie. I know that it is very frightening to step out of oneself, but then everything which is unfamiliar can be frightening. The anonymous girl of this story is so ancient that she could be described as biblical. She was subterranean and had never really flowered. I am telling a lie: she was wild grass.)

Throughout the torrid summers, the oppressive heat of Acre Street made her sweat, a sweat that gave off an appalling stench. A sweat, I couldn't help feeling, that stemmed from sinister origins. Difficult to say if the girl was tubercular. I rather think not. In the night shadows a man was whistling; there were heavy footsteps and the howling of an abandoned mongrel. There were silent constellations, and that space known as time which has nothing to do with her or with us. And so the days passed. The cockerel's crowing in the blood-red dawn gave a new meaning to her withered existence. As day broke, a flock of birds chirped noisily in Acre Street: life sprouted from the ground, jubilant between the paving stones.

Acre Street for living, Lavradio Street for working, the docks for excursions on Sundays. Now and then the lingering sound of a cargo ship's signal that strangely made the heart beat faster, and in between each signal, the consoling though somewhat melancholy cries of the cockerel.

The cockerel belonged to the never-never land. Its cries came from the infinite right up to her bedside, filling her with gratitude. She slept lightly. For the past twelve months she had been suffering from a persistent cold. In the early hours each morning, she was seized by a fit of hoarse coughing, which she tried to smother with her limp pillow. Her room-mates — Maria da Penha, Maria Aparecida, Maria José and plain Maria — paid no attention. They were too exhausted to complain, worn out by an occupation that was no less taxing simply because it was anonymous. One of the girls sold Coty face powder. What a curious occupation! They turned on to their other sides and went back to sleep. The girl's coughing actually lulled them into an even deeper sleep. Is the sky above or below? The girl from the North-east was wondering. As she lay there, she couldn't decide. Sometimes before falling asleep she felt the pangs of hunger and became quite giddy as she visualized a side of beef. The solution was to chew paper into pulp and swallow it. Honestly! I'm getting used to her but I still feel uneasy. Dear God! I feel happier with animals than with people. When I watch my horse cantering freely across the fields — I am tempted to put my head against his soft, vigorous neck and narrate the story of my life. When I stroke my dog on the head — I know that he doesn't expect me to make sense or explain myself.

Perhaps the girl from the North-east has already come to the conclusion that life is troublesome, a soul that doesn't quite match its body, even a delicate soul like hers. Being very superstitious, the girl imagined that if she should ever begin to enjoy life, the spell would be broken. She would cease to be a princess and become transformed into an insect. Because, however awful her situation might be, she had no wish to be deprived of herself. She wanted to be herself. She feared that she would incur some terrible punishment and even be sentenced to death if she began to

31

experience pleasure. So she shielded herself from death by living below par, by consuming her life sparingly so that it shouldn't come to an abrupt ending. This economy provided some reassurance, for the person who falls can only hit the floor. Did she feel that she had nothing to live for? I have no way of knowing, but I think not. Only once did she ask herself that traumatic question: Who am I? The question frightened her to such an extent that her mind became paralysed. I feel, without becoming her, that I have nothing to live for. I am gratuitous, and I pay my bills for electricity, gas and telephone. As for the girl, she would sometimes buy a rose when the boss paid out her wages.

These events belong to the present and I shall only finish this awkward narrative when I am too exhausted to struggle any longer. I am no deserter.

Sometimes the girl remembered the disturbing words of a French ballad. She had heard it sung out of tune by a group of young girls who danced in a circle, joining hands — she had listened without being able to participate because her aunt was calling her to come and sweep the floor. With their, long, wavy hair in pink ribbons, the girls sang: 'Give me one of your daughters . . . maré-marré-deci.' 'I chose your daughter . . . maré-marré.' A pale spectre, the music hovered like a rose of reckless beauty. Yet transient. Pale and transient, the girl was now the sweet and horrifying spectre of a childhood without games or dolls. At such moments, she would pretend that she was running along corridors clutching a doll to her chest and chasing a ball with much laughter and amusement. Her laughter was terrifying because it belonged to the past and it was only revived by a malign imagination, a yearning for what might have been but never was. (I gave you fair warning that this is what is known as popular literature despite my reluctance to betray any emotion.)

It must be said that the girl is not conscious of my presence. Were it otherwise, she would have someone to pray for and that would mean salvation. But I am fully conscious of her presence: through her I utter my cry of horror to existence. To this existence I love so dearly.

To return to the girl: the one luxury she permitted herself was a few sips of cold coffee before going to bed. She paid for this luxury by waking up with heartburn.

She rarely spoke (having little or nothing to say) but she loved sounds. Sounds were life. The night's silence made her feel nervous. It was as if night were about to pronounce some fatal word. At night, cars seldom passed through Acre Street. When they did, the louder their horns the more she liked it. As if these fears were not enough, she was also terrified of catching some dreadful disease down below — that was something her aunt had taught her. Although her tiny ovules were all shrivelled. So hopelessly shrivelled. Her life was so monotonous that by the end of the day she could no longer remember what had happened that same morning. She mused in silence and the thought came to her: since I am, the solution is to be. The cockerel I mentioned earlier heralded yet another day. It sang of weariness. Speaking of poultry, the girl sometimes ate a hard-boiled egg in a snack-bar. Her aunt had always insisted that eggs were bad for the liver. That being so, she obediently became ill and suffered pains on the left side opposite the liver. For the girl was most impressionable. She believed in everything that existed and in everything non-existent as well. But she didn't know how to embellish reality. For her, reality was too enormous to grasp. Besides, the word *reality* meant nothing to her. Nor to me, dear God.

As she slept, she often dreamed that her aunt was rapping her on the head. More surprisingly, she often dreamed about sex, she, who to all appearances was completely asexual. When she finally woke up, she was overcome by feelings of guilt without being able to explain why. Perhaps because everything that is pleasurable should be forbidden. Guilty and contented. Her doubts confirmed her sense of

33

guilt and she mechanically recited three Hail Marys, Amen, Amen, Amen. She prayed but without God. She did not know Him, therefore He did not exist.

Leaving God aside, I have just discovered that reality made little sense to the girl. She felt much more at ease with the unreality of everyday life. She lived in slo-o-ow motion, a hare le-e-eaping through the a-a-air over hi-i-ill and da-a-ale, obscurity was her earth, obscurity was the inner core of nature.

She found consolation in being sad. Not desperate, for she was much too modest and simple to indulge in despair, but that indefinable quality associated with romantics. It goes without saying that she was neurotic. Neurosis sustained her. Dear God, neurosis counted for something: almost as good as crutches. Occasionally she wandered into the more fashionable quarters of the city and stood gazing at the shop windows displaying glittering jewels and luxurious garments in satin and silk — just to mortify the senses. The truth is that she needed to find herself and a little mortification helped.

On Sundays, she always woke up early in order to be able to spend more time doing absolutely nothing. The worst moment of all was late on Sunday afternoons when she would lapse into anxious meditation, the emptiness of barren Sunday. She sighed. She recalled her childhood with nostalgia — dried mandioca — and believed that she had been happy. In truth, no matter how bad one's childhood may have been, it always sounds enchanted in recollection — how awful. The girl never complained about anything. She accepted things as they are — after all, who was responsible for organizing the land inhabited by men? Surely one day she would gain a place in the paradise reserved for misfits. Besides, in her case it simply isn't a question of gaining Paradise. She is a misfit even in this world. I swear that nothing can be done for her. Believe me, I would help her if I could. I realize that in saying that my

34

typist has a diseased body, I am saying something much more offensive than any obscenity.

(It's as good as saying that a healthy dog is worth more.)

At this point, I must record one happy event. One distressing Sunday without mandioca, the girl experienced a strange happiness: at the quayside, she saw a rainbow. She felt something close to ecstasy and tried to retain the vision: if only she could see once more the display of fireworks she had seen as a child in Maceió. She wanted more, for it is true that when one extends a helping hand to the lower orders, they want everything else; the man on the street dreams greedily of having everything. He has no right to anything but wants everything. Wouldn't you agree? There were no means within my power to produce that golden rain achieved with fireworks.

Should I divulge that she adored soldiers? She was mad about them. Whenever she caught sight of a soldier, she would think, trembling with excitement: is he going to murder me?

If the girl only knew that my own happiness stems from the deepest sorrow and that sorrow is an abortive form of happiness. Certainly, she was a contented creature despite the neurosis. The neurosis of battle.

Apart from her monthly visit to the cinema, she enjoyed another luxury. She lacquered her nails a bright scarlet. Unfortunately, she had bitten her nails to such an extent that most of the lacquer had disappeared, revealing the grime underneath.

And when she woke up? When she woke up, she no longer knew her own identity. Only later did she reflect with satisfaction: I am a typist and a virgin, and I like coca-cola. Only then did she get dressed, and spend the rest of the day passively enacting the role of being.

Perhaps I could enhance this story if I were to introduce some difficult technical terms? But that is the problem: this story has no technique, not even in matters of style. It has

35

been written at random. Nothing would persuade me to contaminate with brilliant, mendacious words, a life as frugal as that of my typist. During the day, like everyone else, I make gestures that are unobserved even by me. One of my most unobserved gestures is this story, which comes out as it will, independent of me.

The typist lived in a kind of limbo, hovering between heaven and hell. She had never given any thought to the concept: 'I am, therefore, I am.' I suspect that she felt she had no right to do so, being a mere accident of nature. A foetus wrapped up in newspaper and thrown on to a rubbish dump. Are there thousands of others like her? Yes, thousands of others who are mere accidents of nature. And if one thinks about it carefully, aren't we all mere accidents of nature? I have only escaped from a similar fate because I am a writer. Any action is also a fact. When I make contact with my spiritual forces, I find your God within myself. Why do I write? Can I explain? I simply don't know. In fact, I sometimes think that I am not me. I seem to belong to a remote planet, I am such a stranger unto myself. Can this be me? I am horrified by this encounter with myself.

As I've already said, the girl from the North-east did not believe in death. She couldn't believe in death — after all — was she not alive? She had long since forgotten the names of her father and mother, for her aunt had never mentioned them. (I am exploiting the written word with the utmost ease. This alarms me, for I am afraid of losing my sense of order and of plunging into an abyss resounding with cries and shrieks: the Hell of human freedom. But I shall continue.)

To continue:

Every morning she switched on the transistor radio loaned by one of her room-mates, Maria da Penha. She switched it on as low as possible so as not to disturb the others, and she invariably tuned into Radio Clock, a channel that broadcast the correct time and educational programmes.

There was no music, only a constant ping like drops of falling rain — a drop for every minute that passed. This channel took advantage of the pauses between each ping to broadcast commercials. She adored commercials.

It was the ideal programme for between each ping the announcer gave snippets of information that one day might stand her in good stead. This was how the girl learned, for example, that the Emperor Charlemagne was known as Carolus in his native land. Admittedly, she had never had any opportunity to make use of this information. But you never know. Patience always pays off in the end. Listening to the same programme, she also learned that the only animal that doesn't crossbreed with its own offspring, is the horse.

— That's filth! she muttered to the transistor radio.

On another occasion, she heard the message: 'Repent in Christ and He will give you great joy.' So she decided to repent. Not quite knowing what she had to repent of, the girl from the North-east repented of everything. The preacher added that vengeance is a deadly sin. So she sought no revenge.

Yes, patience always pays off in the end. Seriously? The girl possessed what is known as inner life without knowing that she possessed it. She was nourished by her own entity, as if she were feeding off her own entrails. When she travelled to work, she behaved like a harmless lunatic. As the bus sped along, she daydreamed aloud and voiced the most extravagant dreams. Her dreams were empty on account of all that inner life, because they lacked the essential nucleus of any prior experience of— of ecstasy, let's say. Most of the time, she possessed, without knowing it, the emptiness that replenishes the souls of saints. Was she a saint? It would seem so. The girl didn't know that she was meditating, for the word meditation was unknown to her. I get the impression that her life was one long meditation about nothingness. Except that she needed others in order

37

to believe in herself, otherwise she would become lost in the continuous, spiralling vacuum inside her. She tended to meditate while she typed, and this caused her to make even more mistakes than usual.

She indulged in certain little pleasures. On wintry nights, shivering from head to foot under a thin cotton sheet, she would read by candle-light the advertisements that she had cut out of old newspapers lying around the office. She collected newspaper advertisements, and pasted them into an album. The advertisement she treasured most of all was in colour: it advertised a face cream for women with complexions so very different from her own sallow skin. Blinking furiously (a fatal tic that she had recently acquired), she imagined the pleasure of possessing such luxuries. The cream looked so appetizing that, were she to find enough money to buy it, she wouldn't be foolish. Never mind her skin! She would eat the cream, she would, in large spoonfuls straight from the jar. She was needing to put on some flesh, for her body was drier than a half-empty sack of toasted breadcrumbs. With time, she had become transformed into mere living matter in its primary state. Perhaps this was her protection from the enormous temptation to be unhappy and to feel sorry for herself. (When I consider that I might have been born her — and why not? — I shudder. The fact that I am not her strikes me as being a cowardly escape. I feel remorse, as I explained in one of my titles for this book.)

In any case, the future looked brighter. The future, at least, had the advantage of not being the present, and the worse can always take a turn for the better. There wasn't a trace of human misery in the girl. She carried within her an aura of innocence. For, strange though it may seem, she had faith. Composed of fine organic matter, she existed. Pure and simple. And what about me? The only thing that can be said about me is that I am breathing.

Even though all she possessed within was that tiny essential flame: the breath of life. (I am having a hellish time with this story. May the Gods never decree that I should write about a leper, for then I should become covered in leprosy.) (I am delaying the events that I can vaguely foresee, simply because I need to make several portraits of this girl from Alagoas. Also because if anyone should read this story, I'd like them to absorb this young woman like a cloth soaked in water. The girl embodies a truth I was anxious to avoid. I don't know whom I can blame, but someone is to blame.)

Is it possible that in penetrating the seeds of her existence, I am violating the secrets of the Pharaohs?

Will I be condemned to death for discussing a life that contains, like the lives of all of us, an inviolable secret? I am desperately trying to discover in the girl's existence at least one bright topaz. Perhaps I shall succeed before finishing my story. It's much too early to say, but I am hopeful.

I forgot to mention that sometimes this typist is nauseated by the thought of food. This dates from her childhood when she discovered that she had eaten a fried cat. The thought revolted her for ever more. She lost her appetite and felt the great hunger thereafter. She was convinced that she had committed a crime; that she had eaten a fried angel, its wings snapping between her teeth. She believed in angels, and because she believed in them, they existed. The girl had never eaten lunch or dinner in a restaurant. She ate her food standing at the snack-bar on the street corner. She fancied that a woman who enters a restaurant must be French and on the loose.

There were certain words whose meaning escaped her. One such word was *ephemeris*. For didn't Senhor Raimundo ask her to copy from his elegant handwriting the word *ephemeris* or *ephemerides*? She found the word *ephemerides* altogether mysterious. When she copied the word out she paused over each letter. Her workmate Glória could do shorthand and, not only did she earn more, but she even seemed unperturbed by those difficult words that the boss was so fond of using. Meanwhile, the girl became en-amoured of the word *ephemeris*.

Another portrait: she had never received gifts from any-one. It didn't worry her for she needed so little. One day, however, she saw something that, for one brief moment, she dearly wanted: it was a book that Senhor Raimundo, who was fond of literature, had left on the table. The book was entitled *The Shamed and Oppressed*. The girl remained pensive. Perhaps for the very first time she had established her social class. She thought and thought and thought! She decided that no one had ever really oppressed her and that everything that happened to her was inevitable. It was futile trying to struggle. Why struggle? I ask myself: will she one day experience love and its farewell? Will she one day experience love and its deceptions? Will she experience love's rapture in her own modest way? Who can tell? How can one disguise the simple fact that the entire world is somewhat sad and lonely? The girl from the North-east was lost in the crowd. She caught the bus in Mauá Square. It was bitterly cold and she had no warm clothing to protect her from the wind. But there were the cargo ships that filled her with yearning for who knows what. This happened only on the rare occasion. Most of the time she walked out of her gloomy office into the fading light, and noted that every day at the same hour, it was exactly the same hour. Nothing could be done about the great clock that marked time within time. Yes, to my exasperation, the same hour. Well, so what? So nothing! Speaking for myself, the author of this human character, I cannot stand repetition: routine divides me from potential novelties within my reach.

Speaking of novelties, one day the girl saw a man in a snack-bar who was so amazingly good-looking that she would have loved to take him home. It would be like — like possessing a large emerald — emerald — emerald displayed in a jewel box. Forbidden to touch. The ring on his finger suggested that he was married. How could one marry —

marry — marry a man who was only meant to be seen — seen — seen, she stammered in her mind. She would die of shame were she to eat in his presence, for he was much too good-looking by far.

It occurred to her that she would like to rest her back for just a day. She knew that if she spoke to her boss, he would refuse to believe that her ribs were aching. So she had recourse to a lie that sounded much more convincing than the truth: she informed her boss that she would be unable to turn up for work the following day because she had to have a tooth extracted that might be troublesome. The lie worked. Sometimes only a lie can save you. The following day, therefore, when the four weary Marias set off for work, she could enjoy at long last the greatest privilege of all: solitude. She had the room all to herself. The girl could scarcely believe that all this space was hers to enjoy. It was so quiet you could have heard a pin drop. Overcome with joy at her good fortune, the girl danced with reckless abandon. Her aunt would never have tolerated this behaviour. She danced and waltzed round the room for solitude made her: f-r-e-e! She took full advantage of this well-earned solitude, of the transistor radio which she played at full volume, of the room's spaciousness once vacated by the four Marias. She begged some instant coffee as a special favour from the landlady, then as an additional favour, she also asked for some boiling water. As she drank, licking her lips between each sip, she studied her own enjoyment in the mirror. To confront herself was a pleasure that she had never before experienced. I have never been so happy in my whole life, she thought. She owed nothing to anyone, and no one owed her anything. She even indulged in the luxury of feeling a little weary — a weariness quite unlike the usual weariness.

I am a little suspicious of this sudden ease with which the girl is asking favours. Perhaps she needed special conditions in order to become appealing. Why hadn't she always

41

behaved like this? Even looking at herself in the mirror was no longer quite so alarming: she was contented but how it ached.

— Ah, merry month of May, abandon me no more! (Bang) she exclaimed inwardly the following morning, the seventh of May, she who never exclaimed anything. Probably because she had finally been given something. Given to her by herself, but nevertheless given.

On the morning of the seventh of May, an unforeseen ecstasy gripped her tiny body. The bright, open light from the streets penetrated her opacity. May, the month of bridal veils floating in clouds of white.

What follows is merely an attempt to reproduce three pages which I had already written. My cook, seeing them lying around, threw them into the wastepaper-basket to my utter despair — let the souls in Purgatory assist me to bear the almost unbearable, for the living are not much good to me. This tentative reconstruction is nothing like my original version of the girl's meeting with her future boy friend. Abashed, I shall try to relate the story of the story. But if anyone asks me how it came about, I shall reply: I simply do not know. I've lost the thread of my plot.

May, the month of brides, transformed into butterflies floating in white tulle. Her exclamations could have been a premonition of what was about to occur in the late afternoon of that same day. In a downpour of rain, she met (bang) the first boy-friend of any kind she had ever known, her heart beating furiously as if she had swallowed a little bird that continued to flutter inside her. The boy and the girl stared at each other in the rain and recognized each other as native North-easterners, creatures of the same species with that unmistakable aura. She stared at him, drying her wet face with her hands. The girl only had to see the youth in order to transform him immediately into her guava preserve with cheese.

He . . .

He approached her and spoke with the singsong inton-
ation of the North-easterner that went straight to her heart.
He said
— Excuse me, missy, but would you care to come for a
walk?
— Yes, she replied in confusion and haste, before he
could change his mind.
— If you don't mind my asking, what's your name?
— Macabéa.
—Maca — what?
— Béa, she was forced to repeat.
— Gosh, it sounds like the name of a disease . . . a skin
disease.
— I agree but it's the name my mother gave me because of
a vow she made to Our Lady of Sorrows if I should survive.
For the first year of my life, I wasn't called anything because
I didn't have a name. I'd have preferred to go on being called
nothing instead of having a name that nobody has ever
heard of, yet it seems to suit me — she paused for a moment
to catch her breath before adding shyly and a little downhearted — for as you can see, I'm still here . . . so that's that.
— Even in the backwoods of Paraíba, fulfilling a vow is a
question of honour.
Neither of them knew much about walking out together.
They walked under the heavy rain and lingered in front of
an ironmongers that boasted a wide selection of metal
tubes, containers, nuts and bolts. Macabéa, afraid that the
silence between them might be a warning of imminent
separation, remarked to her newly-found boy-friend:
— I love nuts and bolts. What about you?
The second time they met, the rain had settled into a
steady drizzle and soaked them to the skin. Without even as
much as holding hands, they walked under the drizzle, the
water streaming like tears down Macabéa's face.
The third time they met – Well now, if it isn't raining?
The youth, suddenly dropping that superficial veneer of

politeness that his stepfather had inculcated with some effort, snapped at her:

— All you seem to bring is the rain!

— I'm sorry.

She was already so infatuated, however, that she could no longer do without him in her hunger for love.

On one of the occasions they met, she finally plucked up enough courage to ask him his name.

— Olímpico de Jesus Moreira Chaves — he lied, because his real surname was simply Jesus, a clear indication that he was illegitimate. The youth had been brought up by his stepfather, who had taught him how to ingratiate himself with people in order to get his own way and how to pick up girls.

— I don't understand your name — she said.

— Olímpico?

Macabéa pretended to be very inquisitive while concealing the fact that she had never understood anything the first time round. Aggressive as a fighting cock, Olímpico bristled at her foolish questions, to which he could provide no answers. He retorted impatiently:

— I know what it means, but I'm not telling you!

— That's all right, that's all right, that's all right . . . people don't have to understand what names mean. She understood what desire meant — although she didn't know that she understood. That was how it was: she was starving but not for food, it was a numb sort of pain that rose from her lower abdomen, making the nipples of her breast quiver and her empty arms starved of any embrace came out in goose-pimples. She became overwrought and it was painful to live. At such moments, she would shake with nerves and her workmate Glória would rush to get her a glass of water with sugar.

Olímpico de Jesus was a metal-worker and Macabéa failed to notice that he never once referred to himself as a *worker* but always as a *metallurgist*. Macabéa was delighted with his professional standing just as she was proud of being a typist even if she did earn less than the minimum salary. She and Olímpico had social status. 'Metallurgist and typist' were categories of some distinction. Olímpico's job had the flavour one tastes when smoking a cigarette the wrong way round. His job was to collect the metal rods as they came off the machine and load them on to a conveyor belt. Macabéa never got round to asking him why the rods were put on a conveyor belt. He didn't have such a bad life and he even managed to save some of his wages: he had free shelter at night in a hut that was due for demolition because of his friendship with the night watchman.

Macabéa observed:

— Good manners are the best thing one can inherit.

— As far as I'm concerned, the best inheritance is plenty of money. One day, I'll be a rich man — he rejoined grandly, convinced that he was a demon of power: the strength bleeding in his young limbs.

The one thing he would like to have been was a bull-fighter. He had once witnessed a bullfight at the cinema and he had shivered from head to foot when he saw the bull-fighter extend his red cape. Olímpico had felt no compassion for the bull. What he liked was to see blood.

In the North-east, he had saved week after week to earn enough money to have a perfectly sound canine replaced with a false tooth in glittering gold. A gold tooth gave him some standing in society. Moreover, to have actually killed someone had made him a MAN in capital letters. Olímpico felt no remorse, he was what people in the North-east would call a 'brazen thug'. Olímpico, however, remained unaware that he was also an artist. In his spare time he carved effigies of saints which were so attractive that he decided not to sell them. He carved in the smallest details and, without being disrespectful, he left nothing of the Child Jesus' anatomy to the imagination. As far as Olímpico was concerned, what exists, exists, and Jesus was not only divine but also a man just like him minus the gold tooth.

Olímpico was also interested in local politics. He loved listening to public debates and speeches. Not that he didn't have his own ideas about such matters. He would squat on the ground, rolling a cigarette and thinking hard. Just as he used to squat on the ground in his native Paraíba, his backside suspended in mid-air, while he meditated. He would speak out in a loud voice even if there was no one listening.

— I'm an intelligent chap and one of these days I'll be in politics myself.

After all, didn't he have a gift for making speeches? He possessed that singsong intonation and those unctuous phrases one associates with the man who makes public speeches defending and upholding human rights. After all, was he not destined to become a politician one day? (An event this story does not cover.) And when that day comes, he will expect to be treated with some respect.

Macabéa was undeniably a primitive creature while Olímpico de Jesus saw himself as a man about town, the type of man for whom all doors open.

I am determined to avoid any sentimentality so I shall eliminate, without further ado, any hint of compassion implicit in this story. I should mention that Macabéa had never received a letter in her life. And any telephone calls in the office were always for the boss or for Glória. Macabéa once asked Olímpico if he wouldn't care to telephone her at the office. He made a crushing reply:

— Who wants to listen to you talking nonsense on the telephone?

When Olímpico insisted that one day he would become a politician in his native state of Paraíba, she was astounded and thought to herself: when we get married does that mean that I shall be a politician as well? She didn't fancy the idea

46

because the word 'politician' sounded quite unpleasant. (As I explained, this is not a story about abstractions. Later, I shall probably return to the unnamed sensations, perhaps even the sensations of God Himself. But Macabéa's story must be told or else I shall explode.)

On the rare occasion when the couple actually held a conversation, they invariably discussed food: flour, salted beef, dried meat, brown sugar and molasses. These commodities symbolized their past and made them forget their unhappy childhood because in retrospect, memories of childhood are always bitter-sweet and even provoke a certain nostalgia. Olímpico and Macabéa could have been mistaken for brother and sister, a factor — I've only now realized — that would appear to rule out any possibility of their marrying. I'm not sure that they were aware of this factor. Will they get married? I still don't know. All I know is that they were both ingenuous and altogether insignificant.

No, I'm mistaken. It's now clear that Olímpico was by no means ingenuous, however much the universal victim. It's now clear to me that he was wicked to the core. He enjoyed taking his revenge. Revenge gave him an enormous satisfaction and the strength to go on living. He had more strength than Macabéa, whose guardian angel had deserted her.

In the end, what had to happen would happen. Meantime nothing whatsoever happened, for neither of them knew how to invent happenings. They sat on something free of charge: a bench in the public park. Sitting there, they were indistinguishable from the rest of nothingness. For the greater glory of God.

He — Well.
She — Well what?
He — I only said well!
She — But well what?
He — Let's change the subject. You'll never understand.
She — Understand what?

47

He — Mother of God! Macabéa, let's change the subject at once!

She — What shall we talk about then?

He — About you.

She — Me!

He — Why the fuss? Aren't you a human being? Human beings talk about other human beings.

She — Forgive me, but I don't believe that I am all that human.

He — Everybody's human, dear God!

She — I've never got used to the idea.

He — Never got used to what?

She — I can't explain.

He — So?

She — So what?

He — Look, I'm going. You're a dead loss.

She — I can't help being a dead loss. What do you want me to do about it?

He — You talk a load of rubbish. Try to talk about something . . . anything.

She — I don't know what to talk about.

He — You don't know what?

She — Eh?

He — Look, you're getting on my nerves. Let's just shut up. Agreed?

She — Whatever you say.

He — You're really a hopeless case. As for me, I've been called so many things that I've turned into myself. In the backwoods of Paraíba everybody has heard of Olímpico. And one day the whole world is going to be talking about me.

She — Really?

He — Isn't that what I'm telling you! Don't you believe me?

She — Of course I believe you, I believe you, I believe you. I didn't mean to hurt your feelings.

When she was a little girl, Macabéa had seen a house painted white and pink with a back-yard that boasted a well and water-clock. It was exciting to look down the well. And so this became Macabéa's great ambition: to possess a house one day with its own well. Except that she didn't know how to set about realizing her ambition so she asked Olímpico:

— Can you tell me if anybody can buy a well?

— Look here, hasn't it dawned on you that there aren't any answers to the questions you ask?

She stood there leaning her head to one side like a dove when it's feeling sad.

Once when he talked about getting rich, she asked him:

— Are you sure you're not having visions?

— Go to blazes! You don't trust anybody. Only the fact that you're a virgin stops me from cursing you.

— Don't get upset! They say getting upset can affect your stomach.

— Upset, my foot! Make no mistake, I'm on the way to success. You're the one who should be worrying!

— I don't have any worries. I don't need to be successful.

This was the first time she had ever spoken of herself to Olímpico de Jesus, accustomed as she was to forgetting about herself. Macabéa never broke her routine. She was afraid of inventing situations.

— Did I tell you that they said on the radio that a man who was also a mathematician, wrote a book called *Alice in Wonderland*? They also discussed *elgebra*. What does *elgebra* mean?

— Only queers are interested in things like that, men who've turned into pansies. Excuse the word queer. That's something no decent girl should know about.

— On the radio they discuss 'culture' and use difficult words. For instance, what does 'electronic' mean?

Silence.

— I know what it means but I'm not telling you.

49

— I love to hear the pings as the minutes pass: tic-tac-tic-tac-tic-tac. Radio Clock says that it broadcasts the correct time, culture and commercials. What does culture mean?

— Culture is culture, he replied grudgingly. Why don't you get off my back?

— There are so many things I don't understand. What does 'income per head' mean?

— That's easy, it has something to do with medicine.

— What does Count of Bonfim Street mean? What's a Count? Is that the same as a prince?

— A Count is a Count, for God's sake! Besides, I don't need to know the correct time. I wear a watch.

What he didn't tell Macabéa was that he'd stolen it in a washroom at the factory: another worker had left it over the sink while he was washing his hands. Nobody suspected that Olímpico was very skilful when it came to stealing: needless to say, he didn't wear the watch at work.

— Do you know the best thing I've learned? They said on Radio Clock that we should be glad to be alive. And I am. I also heard some lovely music and I almost wept.

— Was it a samba?

— I believe it was. It was sung by a man called Caruso who they said died a long time ago. His voice was so gentle that it was almost painful to listen to. The music was called *Una Furtiva Lacrima*. I don't know why they couldn't say *lágrima* the way it's said in Brazil.

Una Furtiva Lacrima had been the only really beautiful thing in Macabéa's life. Drying her tears, she tried to sing what she had heard. But Macabéa's voice was as rough and tuneless as the rest of her body. When she heard her own voice, she began to weep. She was weeping for the first time and had never imagined that there was so much water in her eyes. She wept and blew her nose, no longer knowing why she was weeping. She wasn't weeping because of the way she lived: never having known any other way of life, she

50

accepted the fact that her life was 'so' — just like Macabéa's herself.

I also believe she was weeping because the music helped her to perceive that there were other ways of feeling; that there were more delicate forms of existence and certain spiritual refinements. She perceived lots of things that she could not understand. Did the word *aristocracy*, for example, mean some grace that had been granted? Most likely. If that were the case, so be it. She penetrated the vast world of music that required no understanding. Her heart exploded. In the company of Olímpico she suddenly became courageous and, plunging into the mysterious depths of her own being, she said:

— I'm sure I can sing that music. La–la–la–la–la.

— You look like a deaf–mute trying to sing. Your voice is like a broken reed.

— That's because I'm singing for the first time in my life.

She was sure that *lacrima* instead of the Portuguese *lágrima* was an error on the part of the programme announcer. The existence of another language had never occurred to Macabéa, and she was convinced that in Brazil one could only speak Brazilian. Apart from the cargo ships that she could watch on the waterfront every Sunday, she only possessed this music. The ultimate substratum of the music was her only vibration.

The flirtation with Olímpico remained lukewarm. He told her:

— After my sainted mother died, there was nothing to keep me in Paraíba.

— What did she die of?

— Of nothing. Her health gave out.

Olímpico concerned himself with important things but Macabéa only noticed unimportant things such as herself. Just as she noticed a gate that was rusting, twisted, creaking and with its paint peeling off; a gate that led to a number of outhouses that all looked alike and were grouped around a villa. She had observed all this from the bus. The villa was numbered 106 and on a plaque she read the name 'Sunrise'. An attractive name that inspired confidence.

Macabéa found Olímpico very knowledgeable about things. He told her things that she had never heard of before. Once he told her:

— A person's face is the most important thing because the face betrays what that person is thinking: your face is that of somebody who has just tasted a sour apple. I can't abide sad faces. Stop looking so mournful — then he came out with a difficult word — he said: try to change your *demeanour*.

She replied in dismay:

— I can't do anything about my face. But it's only my face that's sad, because I'm really quite happy inside. It's wonderful to be alive, don't you think?

— Sure! But the good life is only for the privileged. I'm one of them. I may look small and skinny but I'm really quite strong and I could lift you off the ground with one arm. Let me show you.

— No, no, there are people watching and they'll start laughing at us!

— Don't be such a ninny, nobody's watching us.

They walked to the corner of the street. Macabéa was overjoyed. He really could lift her up above his head. She shouted gaily:

— This is like flying in an airplane.

That's right! Suddenly he couldn't support her weight on one arm any longer and she fell on her face in the mud, blood spurting from her nostrils. She was tactful, however, and quickly reassured him:

— Don't worry, it's nothing serious.

Having no handkerchief to wipe the mud and blood off her face, Macabéa rubbed her face with the hem of her skirt. She pleaded with him: Please don't look while I'm cleaning my face. No decent girl ever lifts her skirt when there are people watching.

Olímpico was becoming extremely impatient but made no reply. After this little episode, he didn't make any attempt to see her again for days: his pride had been injured.

They eventually bumped into each other again. For quite different reasons they had wandered into a butcher's shop. Macabéa only had to smell raw meat in order to convince herself that she had eaten. What attracted Olímpico, on the other hand, was the sight of a butcher at work with his sharp knife. He envied the butcher and would dearly have liked to be in the trade himself. To cut into raw meat with a sharp knife never failed to get him excited. Both of them walked out of the butcher's shop feeling deeply satisfied. Even so, Macabéa couldn't help wondering what the taste of meat was like. And Olímpico pondered: how does one train to be a butcher? What was the secret? (Glória's father worked in a well-stocked butcher's shop.)

Macabéa spoke:

— I shall miss myself so much when I die.

— Rubbish, when you're dead, you're dead and that's that.

— That's not what my aunt told me.

— Damn your aunt!

— Do you know what I really want to be? A movie-star. I only go to the cinema when the boss pays me my wages. I prefer third-class cinemas because they're much cheaper. I adore movie-stars. Did you know that Marilyn Monroe was the colour of peaches?

— And you're the colour of mud. What makes you think that you've got the face or the body to become a film star?

— Am I really so awful?

— Take a good look at yourself in the mirror.

— I can't stand the sight of blood when I go to the cinema. Honestly, I can't stand it. It makes me feel like vomiting.

— Vomiting or weeping?

— Up till now, thanks be to God, I've managed not to vomit.

— I'll bet! There isn't much milk in this cow.

It was so difficult to think. She didn't know how one set about thinking. Olímpico, on the other hand, was able to think and to use fine words. She would never forget their first meeting when he addressed her as 'missy', and made her feel that she was somebody. Once she became somebody, she even felt justified in buying herself a pink lipstick. Her conversation always sounded hollow. She was remotely aware that she had never uttered the right word. She never referred to 'love' as love, but settled for some vague expression or other.

— Look, Macabéa . . .

— Look where?

— God Almighty! Not 'look' meaning to see, but 'look' meaning I want you to listen! Are you listening to me?

— Every word, every single word!

— How can you be listening to every word, dear God, if I haven't said anything so far! Look, I'm going to treat you to a coffee at the snack-bar. How's that?

— Can I have a drop of milk in my coffee?

— Sure, if it costs the same. If it costs any extra, you pay the difference.

Macabéa didn't cost Olímpico anything. Except on this occasion when he bought her a coffee with milk, to which she added spoonful after spoonful of sugar. So much sugar that she almost vomited, but she managed to hold it down for fear of disgracing herself. She always added spoonfuls of sugar in order to make sure she got value for her money.

On one occasion they visited the Zoological Gardens and Macabéa paid for her own entrance ticket. She was terrified when she saw the animals in their cages. They terrified her and she couldn't make out what they were: why did they exist? When she spotted the rhinoceros, a solid, compact, black shape that moved in slow motion, she got such a shock that she wet her knickers. The rhinoceros was surely one of God's mistakes, she thought, begging His pardon for such blasphemy. She didn't have any special God in mind, it was simply a way of expressing herself. By some divine intervention, Olímpico didn't appear to notice that anything was wrong. She made up a story:

— I'm all wet because I sat on a damp bench.

He showed no reaction. She prayed mechanically, she felt so grateful. It wasn't gratitude to God. Macabéa was only repeating what she had learned as a child.

— The giraffe is so graceful, don't you think?

— Rubbish. You can't talk about animals being graceful.

How she wished she could reach high up into the air like the giraffe. When she realized that her remark about the animals displeased Olímpico, she tried to change the topic of conversation:

— On Radio Clock they used a word that worried me: mimetism.

Olímpico eyed her disapprovingly:

— That's not a nice word for a virgin to be using. Why do you have to keep on asking questions about things that don't concern you? The brothels in the Mangue are full of women who asked far too many questions.

— Is the Mangue a district?

— It's an evil place frequented only by men. This won't sink in, but I'm going to tell you something. A chap can still get a woman on the cheap. You've only cost me a coffee so far. That's your lot. I won't be wasting any more money buying you things. Is that clear?

Macabéa thought to herself: he's right. I don't deserve anything from him because I've wet my knickers.

After their walk in the rain through the Zoological Gardens, Olímpico was no longer the same: he was in a foul temper. Forgetting that he himself was rather silent, as one would expect of someone as virile as Olímpico, he bellowed at her:

— Holy smoke! When are you going to open your mouth to say something?

55

Deeply wounded, Macabéa replied:

— Did you know that the Emperor Charlemagne was called Carolus in his native land! Did you also know that a fly travels so fast that if it were to fly in a straight line it would travel the whole universe in twenty-eight days?

— That's a downright lie!

— No it's not, I swear before God that the announcer said so on Radio Clock.

— Well, I don't believe you.

— May I drop dead this minute if I'm telling a lie. May my father and mother burn in hell, if I were to deceive you.

— You'd better watch out or you will drop dead. Listen to me: are you playing dumb or are you just plain stupid?

— I don't know what I am. I think I'm a little . . . how can I put it? — Honestly, I don't know what I am.

— At least you know that you're called Macabéa?

— That's true. But I don't know what's inside my name. The only thing I know for certain is that I've never had much to offer . . .

— Well, you'd better get it into your thick skull that my name will be in all the papers one day and I'll be famous.

She asked Olímpico:

— Did I tell you that in the street where I live there's a cockerel that sings?

— Why do you have to tell so many lies?

— I swear it, may my mother drop dead if it isn't true!

— Isn't your old girl already dead?

— Oh, so she is . . . How awful . . .

(But what about me? Here I am telling a story about events that have never happened to me or to anyone known to me. I am amazed at my own perception of the truth. Can it be that it's my painful task to perceive in the flesh truths that no one wants to face? If I know almost everything about Macabéa, it's because I once caught a glimpse of this girl with the sallow complexion from the North-east. Her expression revealed everything about her. As for the youth

56

from Paraíba, I must have had his face imprinted on my mind. When one registers a face spontaneously without any preconceptions, that face reveals everything.)

I am now about to efface myself once more and return to my two characters who were transformed by circumstances into two semi-abstract human beings.

I still haven't filled in all the details about Olímpico. He came from the backwoods of Paraíba. His determination to survive stemmed from his roots in a region noted for its primitive, savage way of life, its recurring spells of drought. Olímpico had arrived in Rio with a tin of perfumed vaseline and a comb, his sole possessions purchased at an open market in Paraíba. He rubbed the vaseline into his hair until it was wet and glossy. It never occurred to him that the girls in Rio might be put off by that lank, greasy hair. He had been born looking more shrivelled and scorched than a withered branch or a stone lying in the sun. Olímpico had a better chance of surviving than Macabéa, for it wasn't by accident that he had killed a rival in the heart of the backwoods: his long, sharp knife had punctured his victim's soft liver with the greatest ease. He had kept this crime a secret, and he enjoyed that sense of power which secrecy can bestow. Olímpico had proved his manliness in combat. Yet he lost all courage when it came to attending funerals: sometimes he attended as many as three funerals a week; the funerals of complete strangers whose names appeared in the obituary columns of *O Dia*. As he read them, his eyes would fill with tears. It showed weakness on his part, but everyone has some weakness or other. A week that passed without a funeral left Olímpico feeling empty. It sounds like madness, but Olímpico knew precisely what he was after. He wasn't the least bit mad. Macabéa, unlike Olímpico, was a crossbreed between one 'quiddity' and another. Truly she seemed to have been conceived from some vague notion in the minds of starving parents. Olímpico at least stole, whenever he had the opportunity, even from the watchman at the factory who provided him with shelter. To have killed someone and to have stolen meant that he was no mere accident of nature. His crimes gave him prestige and made him a man whose honour had already been purged. He had an additional advantage over Macabéa. Olímpico had a considerable talent for drawing instant caricatures of well-known personalities, whose photographs regularly appeared in the press. This was his revenge. His only act of kindness toward Macabéa was his offer to get her a job in the metal factory, should she be given the sack. His offer made her deliriously happy (bang) for in the metal factory she would find her only real connection with the world: Olímpico. Macabéa didn't worry too much about her own future: to have a future was a luxury. She had learned from her favourite radio programme that there were seven billion inhabitants in the world. She felt completely lost. But it was in her nature to be happy so she soon resigned herself: there were seven billion inhabitants to keep her company.

Macabéa had a passion for horror films and musicals. She especially liked films where the women were hanged or shot through the heart with a bullet. It never dawned on her that she herself was a suicide case even though she had never contemplated killing herself. Her life was duller than plain bread and butter. By contrast, Olímpico was a demon of strength and vitality who had fathered children. He possessed the precious semen in abundance. And as was said or left unsaid, Macabéa had ovaries as shrivelled as overcooked mushrooms. Oh, if only I could seize Macabéa, give her a good scrubbing and a plate of hot soup, kiss her on the forehead and tuck her up in bed. So that she might wake up to discover the great luxury of living.

Olímpico — as I now discover — derived little satisfaction from courting Macabéa. Olímpico probably realized that Macabéa lacked substance like most inferior products. However, when he set eyes on Glória, Macabéa's workmate, he felt at once that here was a girl with real class.

Glória had rich Portuguese wine in her blood and a provocative way of swinging her hips as she walked, no doubt due to some remote strain of African blood. Although she was white, Glória displayed that vitality one associates with a mulatta. She dyed her curly mop of hair bright yellow though the roots remained dark. But even without the peroxide she was fair, and that made her superior as far as Olímpico was concerned. This was a point in her favour no North-easterner could ignore. And when Glória was introduced to him by Macabéa, she assured him: 'I'm *carioca* born and bred!' Olímpico had never heard the expression 'born and bred', an expression that had been popular in Rio when Glória's parents were children. To be *carioca* identified Glória with the privileged class who inhabited Southern Brazil. Looking closely at her, Olímpico perceived at once that, although she was ugly, Glória was well nourished. This was enough to transform her into someone of quality.

In the meantime, his affair with Macabéa waned into a lukewarm routine. Not that one could ever have described it as being warm. More and more often he failed to turn up at the bus stop. But at least he was still her boy-friend. Macabéa anxiously awaited the day when he would finally propose that they should become engaged. And marry.

Olímpico soon learned in a roundabout way that Glória had a father and mother, and that she ate a hot meal at the same hour every day. These details transformed her into someone of first-class quality. Olímpico was thrilled when he found out that Gloria's father worked in a butcher's shop. Watching those hips, Olímpico could see that Glória was made for bearing children. Macabéa, by comparison, had all the signs of her own unmistakable doom.

It was quite alarming to observe how the breath of life surged within Macabéa's parched body; expansive and diffused, and as abundant as the breath of a pregnant woman, impregnated by herself, by parthenogenesis: she experienced the weirdest dreams with visions of immense prehistoric animals, as if she were living in some more remote age of this violent territory.

At this point (bang), the affair between Olímpico and Macabéa came to an abrupt end. It had been a curious affair yet was somehow akin to the paler shades of love. Olímpico bluntly informed her that he had met another girl and that the other girl in question was Glória. (Bang) Macabéa saw at once what had happened between Olímpico and Glória: their eyes had met and kissed.

Confronted with Macabéa's vacant expression, Olímpico was almost tempted to offer some words of comfort before saying goodbye. As he was about to take his leave, he quipped:

— Macabéa, you're like a hair in one's soup. It's enough to make anyone lose their appetite. I don't want to hurt your feelings, but you might as well know the truth. Are you offended?

— No, no, no! Please leave me alone! Say goodbye and go!

It is better not to speak of happiness or unhappiness — such words provoke that vague nostalgia suffused in lilac, the perfume of violets, those gelid tidal waters that send spray over the sands. I have no desire to provoke any of these things for they are painful.

I forgot to mention that Macabéa had one unfortunate trait: she was sensual. How could there be so much sensuality in a body as withered as hers, without her even suspecting its presence? A mystery. At the outset of her affair with Olímpico, she had asked him for a small photograph, three by four centimetres, which showed him smiling broadly and showing off his gold tooth. She was so excited when he gave it to her that she said three Our Fathers and two Hail Marys to recover her composure.

When Olímpico told her the affair was over, her reaction (bang) was immediate and totally unexpected: she suddenly started laughing. She laughed because she had forgotten how to weep. Surprised and puzzled, Olímpico went into hoots of laughter.

The two of them stood there laughing. At that moment, Olímpico had an intuition, that came close to being an act of kindness: he asked Macabéa if she was laughing because she felt nervous. She stopped laughing, and suddenly feeling very, very tired, she replied: I don't really know . . .

Macabéa, however, knew one thing: Glória was the embodiment of vigorous existence. This was probably due to the fact that Glória was buxom. Macabéa had always secretly longed to be buxom, after hearing a young man in Maceió say to a girl who was passing by; 'You're a buxom beauty!' From that moment onwards, she had studied ways and means of putting on some flesh. She even summoned enough courage to ask her aunt to buy her some cod liver oil. (Already addicted to advertisements, she had read about cod liver oil.) Her aunt rebuked her: Who do you think you are, some rich man's daughter, accustomed to luxuries?

Since it was not in her nature to be downhearted, she tried to carry on after Olímpico abandoned her as if nothing had happened. (She felt no despair, etc. etc.) Besides, what else could she do? She was a lost cause. And even sadness was the privilege of the rich, of those who could afford it, of those who had nothing better to do. Sadness was a luxury.

I should also mention that on the day after Olímpico abandoned her, Macabéa had an idea. Since nobody wanted to give her a treat, much less become engaged to her, she would give herself a treat. The treat would consist of buying a new lipstick she didn't really need: not pink like the one she was using, but this time bright red. In the washroom at the office she painted her lips lavishly beyond their natural outline, in the hope that she might achieve that stunning effect seen on the lips of Marilyn Monroe. When she had finished, she stood staring at herself in the mirror, at a face which stared back in astonishment. The thick lipstick looked like blood spurting from a nasty gash, as if someone had punched her on the mouth and broken her front teeth (small bang). When she went back to her desk Glória chuckled:

— Have you taken leave of your senses, girl? What are you up to, wearing all that war-paint? You could be mistaken for a tart.

— I'm a virgin! You won't find me going out with soldiers or sailors.

— Excuse my asking: is it painful being ugly?

— I've never really thought about it, I suppose it's a little painful. How do you feel about it being ugly yourself?

— I am not ugly! — Glória howled at her.

Peace was soon restored between them, and Macabéa continued to be happy thinking about nothing. Empty, empty. As I said before, she had no guardian angel. But she made the best of things. Beyond that, she was almost impersonal. Glória probed:

— Why are you always asking me for aspirin? I don't grudge you the odd aspirin, but pills cost money.

— To stop the pain.

— What do you mean? Eh? Are you in pain?

— I'm in pain all the time.

— Where?

— Inside. I can't explain it.

More and more, she was finding it difficult to explain. She had transformed herself into organic simplicity. She had contrived a way of finding grace in simple, authentic things. She liked to feel the passage of time. She did not possess a watch, and perhaps for that very reason, she relished the infinity of time. Her life was supersonic. Yet no one noticed that she had crossed the sound barrier with her existence. For other people, she didn't exist. Her only advantage over others was to know how to swallow pills at one go, without any water. Glória, who supplied her with aspirin, was full of admiration and this kindled a pleasing warmth in Macabéa's heart. Glória warned her:

62

— One of these days the aspirin will stick in your throat and you'll be running around the office like a beheaded chicken.

One day Macabéa enjoyed a moment of ecstasy. It happened in front of a tree that was so enormous that she couldn't put her arms around its trunk. Yet despite her ecstasy, she did not abide with God. She prayed with total indifference. True. Yet that mysterious God of others sometimes bestowed on her a state of grace. Bliss, bliss, bliss. Her soul almost took flight. She, too, had become a flying saucer. She had tried to confide in Glória but decided against it. She didn't know how to express herself and what was there to confide? The atmosphere? One doesn't confide everything, for everything is a hollow void.

Sometimes, grace descended upon her as she sat at her desk in the office. Then she would go to the washroom in order to be alone. Standing and smiling until it passed. (It strikes me that this God was extremely merciful towards her: He restored what He had taken from her.) Standing and thinking about nothing, a vacant expression in her eyes.

Not even Glória could be called a friend: just a workmate. Glória, who was buxom, white and tepid. Her body exuded a peculiar smell, and it was quite obvious that she didn't wash much. She bleached the hairs on her legs and under the armpits without bothering to shave them. Olímpico wondered: was she bleached down below as well?

Towards Macabéa, Glória felt vaguely maternal. Whenever she saw Macabéa looking more shrivelled than usual, she would chide her:

— Why are you looking like . . . ?

Macabéa, who never lost her temper with anyone, had to control her impatience with Glória, who had this irritating habit of never finishing a sentence. Glória used an overpowering cologne that smelled of sandalwood, and Macabéa, who had a delicate stomach, always felt queasy when she inhaled the odour. She preferred to say nothing because Glória was now her only remaining contact with the world. A world that consisted of her aunt, Glória, Senhor Raimundo and Olímpico — and more remotely, the girls with whom she stared a room. To compensate, she identified with a portrait of the young Greta Garbo. This surprised me, for I could not imagine any affinity between Macabéa and an actress with a face like Garbo. Although she couldn't explain it, Macabéa was convinced that Garbo was the most important woman in the world. She herself felt no inclination to be like the haughty Greta Garbo, whose tragic sensuality placed her on a solitary pedestal. What Macabéa wanted most of all, as I've already said, was to look like Marilyn Monroe.

She rarely confided in anyone, but one day she made the mistake of telling Glória about her secret ambition. Glória burst out laughing:

— You, Maca, looking like Marilyn Monroe? Have you seen yourself in the mirror?

Glória was terribly smug: in her own estimation, she thought of herself as being really something. Conscious of her mulatta sex appeal, she painted in a beauty spot above her lips, to add a touch of glamour to the bleached hairs around her mouth. Glória was a cunning vixen but none the less good-hearted. Macabéa's situation worried her, but there was little she could do to improve matters. After all, no one forced Macabéa to be quite so foolish? And as Glória reminded herself: she's not my responsibility.

No one can enter another's heart. Macabéa conversed with Glória — without ever opening her heart.

Glória wiggled her bottom in an inviting way and she smoked mentholated cigarettes to keep her breath fresh for those interminable kissing sessions with Olímpico. She was very self-confident, having achieved most of her modest ambitions in life. There was a defiant note in Glória's attitude as if to say: 'Nobody bosses me around.' One day she suddenly began to stare and stare and stare at Macabéa.

Until she couldn't keep silent any longer and, speaking with the slightest trace of Portuguese ancestry in her accent, she said:

— Hey girl, haven't you any face?

— Of course I have a face. It's just that my nose is flat. After all, I'm from Alagoas.

— Tell me something: do you ever think about your future?

The question remained unanswered, for Macabéa had nothing to say.

Very well. Let us return to Olímpico.

In an attempt to impress Glória and play the macho, he bought red hot peppers at the market frequented by North-easterners, and to show his new girl-friend just how tough he was, he bit right into the devil's fruit. He didn't even drink a glass of water to quell the burning sensation. The unbearable pain made him feel tough and a terrified Glória suddenly became submissive. He thought to himself: I'm a conqueror, after all. And he attacked Glória with the ferociousness of a male bee, craving for her honey and that succulent flesh. He felt no remorse for having ditched Macabéa. He was destined to go up in the world and join the privileged. Olímpico was determined to change his life. By associating with Glória, this insignificant metal-worker from the North-east was about to prosper. He would cease to be what he had always been and what he had always refused to acknowledge, ashamed of his own weakness. Even as a child he had been a lonely creature who found it difficult to breathe in space. The man from the backwoods is, above all, patient. I find it easy to forgive him.

Glória, wishing to make amends for having stolen her boy friend, invited Macabéa to tea one Sunday afternoon at her parents' house. Kissing the wound better after biting someone? (This story is so banal that I can scarcely bear to go on writing.)

This invitation (small bang) caused Macabéa to open her

65

eyes wide. In the foul disorder of a third-class surburban bourgeoisie one could still count upon eating well, for most of their money was spent on food. Glória lived in a street named after some General or other. It gave her enormous satisfaction to be able to say that she lived in a street that commemorated a military leader. This made her feel much more secure. In Glória's house there was even a telephone. This was probably one of the few occasions when Macabéa realized why there was no place for her in this world and why Glória was being so generous. A cup filled to the brim with piping hot chocolate mixed with real milk, a selection of sugared buns and even a small cake. While Glória was out of the room, Macabéa furtively ate a biscuit. She then asked to be forgiven by the Abstract Being, the Giver and Taker of all things. She felt she had been forgiven. The Abstract Being had shown mercy.

On the following day, which was a Monday, perhaps because the chocolate had affected her liver or because of her nervousness about drinking something intended for the rich, Macabéa felt unwell.

With an act of will-power, she prevented herself from vomiting in her determination not to squander that delicious chocolate. Some days later, when she received her wages, she summoned enough courage for the first time in her life (bang) to make an appointment with a doctor recommended by Glória, who didn't charge much. He examined her, examined her a second time, and then a third time.

— Are you dieting to lose weight, my girl?
Macabéa didn't know how to reply.
— What do you eat?
— Hot dogs.
— Is that all?
— Sometimes I eat a mortadella sandwich.
— What do you drink? Milk?
— Only coffee and soft drinks.

— What do you mean by soft drinks? — He probed, not quite knowing how to proceed. He questioned her at random:

— Do you sometimes have fits of vomiting?

— Oh, never! — she exclaimed in a panic, for she was not a fool to go wasting food, as I've explained. The doctor took a good look at her and felt sure that she didn't diet to lose weight. Nevertheless, he found it easier to go on insisting that she shouldn't diet to lose weight. He knew how things stood and that he was the poor man's doctor. That was what he muttered to himself as he prescribed a tonic that Macabéa wouldn't even bother to buy: she believed it was sufficient to consult a doctor in order to be cured. He snapped at her without being able to account for his sudden outburst of annoyance and indignation:

— This tale about a diet of hot dogs is pure neurosis. What you need is a psychiatrist!

She had no idea what he was talking about but felt that the doctor expected her to smile. So she smiled.

The doctor, who was corpulent and given to perspiring, suffered from a nervous tic that caused him to purse his lips at regular intervals. As a result, he looked like a pouting infant about to burst into tears.

This doctor had no ambition whatsoever. He saw medicine simply as a means of earning a living. It had nothing to do with dedication or concern for the sick. He was negligent and found the squalor of his patients utterly distasteful. He resented having to deal with the poor whom he saw as the rejects of that privileged society from which he himself had been excluded. It had not escaped him that he was out of touch with the latest trends in medicine and new clinical methods, but he had all the training he was likely to need for treating the lower orders. His dream was to earn enough money to do exactly what he pleased: nothing.

When the doctor told Macabéa that he was about to give her a medical examination, she said:

— I've been told you have to take your clothes off when you visit a doctor, but I'm not taking anything off.

He gave her an X-ray and said:

— You're in the early stages of pulmonary tuberculosis.

Macabéa didn't know if this was a good or a bad thing. But being ever so polite she simply said:

— Many thanks.

The doctor resisted any temptation to be compassionate. He advised her: when you can't decide what you should eat, make yourself a generous helping of Italian spaghetti.

With a mere hint of kindness in his voice, since he, too, had been treated unjustly by fate, he added:

— It doesn't cost that much . . .

— I've never heard of the food you've just mentioned. Is it good?

— Of course, it is! Just look at this paunch! It comes from eating big helpings of spaghetti and drinking lots of beer. Forget the beer. You had better avoid alcohol.

She repeated wearily:

— Alcohol?

— Shall I tell you something? I wish you'd get the hell out of here!

Yes, I adore Macabéa, my darling Maca. I adore her ugliness and her total anonymity for she belongs to no one. I adore her for her weak lungs and her under-nourished body. How I should like to see her open her mouth and say:

— I am alone in the world. I don't believe in anyone for they all tell lies, sometimes even when they're making love. I find that people don't really communicate with each other. The truth comes to me only when I'm alone.

Maca, however, never expressed herself in sentences, first of all, because she was a person of few words. She wasn't conscious of herself and made no demands on anyone. Maca even thought of herself as being happy. She was no idiot yet she possessed the pure happiness of idiots. She did not think about herself: she lacked self-awareness. (I can

68

see that I've tried to impose my own situation on Maca: I need several hours of solitude every day, otherwise *I die*.)

Speaking for myself, I am only true when I'm alone. As a child, I always feared that I was about to fall off the face of the earth at any minute. Why do the clouds keep afloat when everything else drops to the ground? The explanation is simple: the gravity is less than the force of air that sustains the clouds. Clever, don't you think? Yes, but sooner or later they fall in the form of rain. That is my revenge.

She didn't confide any of this to Glória because on the whole she told lies: she was ashamed of the truth. A lie was so much more acceptable. Macabéa believed that to be well-educated was the same as knowing how to tell lies. She also lied to herself in daydreams that reflected her envy of her work-mate. Glória, for instance, could be so imaginative. Macabéa watched her saying goodbye to Olímpico. Glória would put her finger-tips to her lips and blow a kiss into the air like someone giving a bird its freedom. Such a gesture would never have occurred to Macabéa.

(This story consists of nothing more than some crude items of primary material that come to me directly before I even think of them. I know lots of things that I cannot express. Besides, where does thinking come into it?)

Glória, perhaps because she was feeling remorseful, said to Macabéa:

— Olímpico is mine, but you are sure to find yourself another boy friend. I know that Olímpico is mine because the fortune-teller told me so. I mustn't ignore what she told me for she's a clairvoyante and never makes mistakes. Why don't you pay for a session and ask her to read your cards?

— Does it cost much?

69

I have grown weary of literature: silence alone comforts me. If I continue to write, it's because I have nothing more to accomplish in this world except to wait for death. Searching for the word in darkness. Any little success invades me and puts me in full view of everyone. I longed to wallow in the mud. I can scarcely control my need for self-abasement, my craving for licentiousness and debauchery. Sin tempts me, forbidden pleasures lure me. I want to be both pig and hen, then kill them and drink their blood. I think about Macabéa's vagina, minute, yet unexpectedly covered with a thick growth of black hairs — her vagina was the only vehement sign of her existence.

She herself asked for nothing, but her sex made its demands like a sunflower germinating in a tomb. As for me, I feel weary. Perhaps of keeping company with Macabéa, Glória and Olímpico. That doctor made me feel quite sick with his talk about beer. I must interrupt this story for three days.

Now I awaken to find that I miss Macabéa. Let's take up the threads again.

— Is it very dear?

— I'll loan you the money. Madame Carlota has the power to break any spells that might be worrying her clients. She broke mine on the stroke of midnight on Friday the thirteenth of August over at San Miguel, on a pitch where they practise voodoo. They bled a black pig and seven white hens over me and tore my bloodstained clothes to shreds. Can you pluck up enough courage?

— I don't know if I could stomach all that blood.

Perhaps because blood is everyone's secret, that life-giving tragedy. But Macabéa only knew that she could not stomach the sight of blood, the other reflections were mine. I am becoming interested in facts: facts are solid stones. There is no means of avoiding them. Facts are words expressed throughout the world.

Well then.

Faced with this sudden offer of help, Macabéa, who never remembered to ask for anything, asked her boss for time off by pretending she had toothache. She accepted a loan from Glória without having the faintest idea when she would be able to pay her back. This bold decision surprisingly encouraged her to make an even bolder decision (bang): since the money was on loan, she reasoned somewhat perversely, and was not strictly hers, then she was free to spend it. So for the first time in her life she took a taxi and asked to be dropped in Olaria. I suspect that she acted so boldly out of sheer desperation, even though she didn't know that she was desperate. She was at the end of her tether and felt completely worn out.

Tracing Madame Carlota's address turned out to be straightforward: so very straightforward that Macabéa thought of it as being a favourable omen. Madame Carlota's ground-floor apartment was situated on the corner of a cul-de-sac. On the pavement tiny blades of grass sprouted between the flagstones — Macabéa noticed them because she always noticed things that were tiny and insignificant. She thought dreamily, as she rang the doorbell: grass is so easy and simple. Her thoughts were gratuitous and unconnected because, however erratic, she possessed vast reserves of inner freedom.

It was Madame Carlota herself who came to the door. She greeted Macabéa amiably and said:

— My guiding spirit has already informed me of your visit, my dear. What is your name again? Ah, yes! A very pretty name. Come in, my pet. There is a client with me in the other room. If you don't mind waiting in here. Would you care for a coffee, my pet?

Macabéa was taken aback, never having received so many endearments from anyone. Mindful of her own frail existence, she cautiously sipped the cold coffee which tasted quite bitter. Meantime, she examined with admiration and respect the room in which she was being kept waiting. It all seemed very luxurious. The chairs and settees were covered in yellow plastic. And there were even plastic flowers. Plastic was the last word in luxury. Macabéa sat with her mouth wide open.

Eventually, a young girl emerged from the back room, her eyes red from weeping, and Madame Carlota beckoned Macabéa to enter. (How tiresome to have to grapple with facts. Everyday matters annihilate and I'm not in the mood for writing this story which is merely a form of catharsis. I see that I am writing here and there about myself. I accept no responsibility for what I am writing.)

Let's continue then, however much effort it requires: Madame Carlota was voluptuous; she painted her rosebud mouth a vivid scarlet and dabbed her plump little cheeks with rouge, which became shiny when applied to her greasy complexion. Madame Carlota looked like a large china doll that had seen better days. (I can see that my story lacks depth. I find it exhausting to have to describe things.)

— Don't be frightened, my pet. Anyone at my side is also at the side of Jesus.

Madame Carlota pointed at the coloured print on the wall which represented the Sacred Heart of Jesus in red and gold.

— I'm a fan of Jesus. I'm just mad about Him. He has always helped me. Mind you, in my heyday I had enough class to live the life of a lady. Things were easier then, thanks to Jesus. Later on, when I didn't rate quite so highly on the market, Jesus lost no time in helping me to set up a brothel with a friend. That earned me enough money to buy this ground-floor apartment. I then gave up the brothel for it wasn't easy looking after all those girls who spent most of their time cheating me out of money. Are you interested in what I'm telling you?

— Very.

— Wise girl, for I'm not lying. You should become a fan of Jesus, too, because the Saviour truly redeems. The police clamp down on fortune-telling and accuse me of taking advantage of my clients, but as I said before, not even the police can get rid of Jesus. You have seen how Jesus even provided me with money to buy all this expensive furniture?

— Yes, Madame.

— Ah, so you agree? I could tell right away that you're a bright girl, and, just as well, because it was having my wits about me that saved me.

As she spoke, Madame Carlota extracted one chocolate after another from an open box and popped them into her tiny mouth. She made no attempt to offer one to Macabéa. Macabéa who, as I mentioned, tended to notice the smallest detail, observed that inside every chocolate Madame Carlota bit into, there was a thick cream filling. She did not covet Madame Carlota's chocolates for Macabéa had discovered that things belonged to others.

— I was poor, I had nothing to eat, no decent clothes to wear. So I became a prostitute. I quite enjoyed the work for I'm a very affectionate woman, and I became very fond of all my clients. Besides, life was good in the red-light district. There was a great deal of friendship among the prostitutes. We were a closely-knit community, and only very rarely did I fight with any of the other girls. The quarrels were enjoyable, too, for I was a sturdy lass and I enjoyed punching, biting and pulling the hair of anyone who crossed me. Speaking of biting, you can't imagine what lovely teeth I once had, all white and sparkling. Alas, they rotted so badly that I'm left with dentures. Can you tell that my teeth are false?

— No, Madame.

— You know, I was very fussy about my appearance and I never caught any diseases. Well, I did have syphilis once, but a dose of penicillin soon cured me. I was more understanding than the other prostitutes because I'm very kind-hearted. After all, what I was giving was mine to give. I had a man whom I really adored and whom I kept for he was very genteel and didn't want to soil his lovely hands. He was my little luxury, and sometimes I even used to let him give me a good thrashing. Whenever he gave me a thrashing, I could tell that he was genuinely fond of me and I enjoyed being thrashed. With him it was love, with the other men simply a job. After he disappeared, I took up with another woman to try and forget him. To be loved by another woman is really rather nice. It would even be preferable in your case because you're much too delicate to cope with the brutality of men. If you can find yourself a woman friend, you'll soon find out how nice it can be. Love between two women is more affectionate. Is there any chance of you finding yourself a woman friend?

— No, Madame.

— You ought to do something about your appearance, dearie. Without a touch of glamour, you don't stand a chance. How I miss the red-light district. I knew the Mangue when it was at its best and frequented by real gentlemen. I earned lots of tips, in addition to the fixed rate. They tell me the Mangue is finished and that there are only about six brothels left. I used to stand in the doorway wearing nothing except panties and a bra made of transparent lace. Later on, when I put on weight and started losing my teeth, I decided to run my own brothel. Do you know what the word brothel means? I always use that word because I've never been frightened of words. There are some people who get all worked up if you mention certain words. Are you frightened of words, my pet?

— Yes, Madame, I am.

— Don't worry, dear. I'll try not to shock you with swear words. They tell me that the Mangue smells something terrible these days. In my time, people burned incense to make the place smell nice. The brothel used to smell like the inside of a church. And people were decent and very devout. When I was on the game, I saved quite a bit of money. The woman who managed the brothel took her percentage, of course. Now and then, there were ugly scenes and even gun fights, but I was never involved. Tell me, flower, am I boring you with the story of my life? No? Are you sure? Have you the patience to wait just a little longer before I start reading your fortune?

— Of course, Madame Carlota.

Madame Carlota then went on to tell her how prettily she had decorated the walls of her little cubicle in the brothel in the Mangue.

— Have you ever been told what a nice smell men have, my pet? It's good for one's health. Have you ever experienced a man's smell?

— No, Madame Carlota.

Finally, after licking her lips, Madame Carlota ordered Macabéa to divide the cards with her left hand. With your left hand, is that clear, my little one?

Macabéa divided the pack with a trembling hand: for the first time in her life, she was about to know her destiny. Madame Carlota (bang) was to be the climax of her existence. The vortex of her life as it was about to be channelled into that voluptuous odalisque whose complexion shone like plastic under the bright rouge. Madame Carlota opened her eyes wide.

— Poor little Macabéa, what a terrible life you have! May my friend Jesus have pity on you, my child! How awful!

Macabéa turned pale: it had never occurred to her that her life was so awful.

Madame Carlota divined everything about Macabéa's past, and even revealed that she had never really known her own father and mother and that she had been brought up by a relative who had been as wicked as any stepmother. Macabéa was horrified by these revelations. She had always believed that her aunt had treated her badly for her own good. Madame Carlota went on to say:

— As for your immediate future, my child, that's miserable as well. You're about to lose your job just as you've already lost your boy-friend, you poor little thing. If you haven't got the money to pay me, don't you worry. I'm a woman of some means.

Macabéa, unaccustomed as she was to receiving any favours, turned down this generous offer but with a grateful heart.

Whereupon (bang) something happened out of the blue: Madame Carlota's face suddenly lit up:

— Macabéa! I have some wonderful news for you! Listen carefully, my flower, because what I'm about to tell you is of the greatest importance. It is something very serious and very cheerful: your life is about to change completely! And something else: it will change the very minute you leave this house! You will feel like a new person. And you can be sure, my little one, that even your boy-friend will come back to you and ask you to marry him, for he now regrets having left you! And your boss is about to inform you that he's thought matters over and no longer has any intention of giving you the sack!

Macabéa had never had the courage to cherish hopes. Yet she now listened to Madame Carlota as if she were listening to a fanfare of trumpets coming from heaven — her heart beating furiously. Madame was right: at long last, Jesus was taking some interest in her. Macabéa's eyes opened wide as she felt a sudden hunger for the future (bang). And I, too, am beginning to cherish hope at last.

— Oh, there is something else! You are about to come in for a great fortune that a foreign gentleman will bring to you in the night. Do you know any foreign gentleman?

— No, Madame Carlota — Macabéa replied, beginning to feel disheartened.

— Then you are about to meet one. He is fair, with eyes that could be blue or green or brown or black. And were it not for the fact that you are in love with your former boy friend, this foreigner would fall in love with you. No! No! No! I can see something else (bang) and though I cannot see it very clearly, I can also hear the voice of my guiding spirit: this foreigner is apparently called Hans, and he is the man whom you will marry! He has lots of money, but then all foreigners are rich. Unless I'm mistaken, and I never make mistakes, he is going to show you a great deal of affection: and you, my poor little orphan, you will be dressed in satin and velvet, and you will even be presented with a fur coat!

Macabéa began (bang) to tremble all over, for there is a painful side to a surfeit of happiness. The only answer she could think of:

— I don't need a fur coat in this climate.

— Well, you're going to have one just the same. There's nothing like a fur coat to make a girl look chic. It's a long time since I've read such good cards. I'm always frank with my clients. For example, I've just told that girl you saw leaving that she's going to be knocked down on the road. She wept buckets. Didn't you notice how red her eyes were? I'm going to give you a charm that you must wear tucked into your bra and against your skin. You've no bust, poor thing, but you'll start to fill out. Until you put on a little weight, stuff some cotton-wool into your bra to give the impression that you've got some shape. Listen, pet, I'm afraid I must charge you for the charm in the name of Jesus, because all my earnings as a fortune-teller are donated to an orphanage. But if you haven't got the money on you, don't worry, you can pay me when all the things I've foreseen finally came true.

— No, I'd rather pay you right away. You've guessed everything about me, you're . . .

Macabéa felt almost inebriated and could scarcely gather her thoughts. It was as if someone had delivered a sharp blow to that head of lank hair. Macabéa felt totally confused as if some great misfortune had befallen her.

Most of all, she was experiencing for the first time what other people referred to as passion: she was passionately in love with Hans.

— What can I do to get my hair to grow? — she bravely asked Madame Carlota, now that she was feeling like a new person.

— That's asking too much. But let me see: wash your head with a good shampoo and never use hard soap. There's no charge for that advice.

This as well? (bang) Macabéa's heart thumped furiously at the thought of seeing her hair grow. She had put Olímpico from her mind and could only think of the foreign gentleman: it was almost too good to be true that she should find herself a man with eyes that were blue or green or brown or black. She couldn't go wrong. The range of possibilities was endless.

— And now — said Madame Carlota — you must go off in search of that wonderful destiny. I have another client waiting outside. Besides, I've given you extra time, dearie, but it was worth it!

In a moment of impulse (bang) that was both eager and awkward, Macabéa planted a resounding kiss on Madame Carlota's rouged cheek. Once again, she sensed that her life was suddenly taking a turn for the better. As a little girl, because she had no one to kiss, she often used to kiss the wall. Embracing the wall was like embracing herself.

Madame Carlota had guessed everything and Macabéa was horrified. Only now did she recognize that her life had been miserable. She felt like weeping as she perceived the other side. For as I've already stated, until this moment, Macabéa had thought of herself as being happy.

She walked out of Madame Carlota's apartment in a daze, paused in the cul-de-sac that was already darkening in the twilight — the twilight that belongs to no one. Her eyes dimmed over as if the dying light was a stain of blood and gold already turning to black. The atmosphere seemed charged with riches and the face of descending night — oh, yes — appeared deep and magnificent. Macabéa stood there in bewilderment, uncertain whether she should cross the street now that her life had been transformed. Transformed, moreover, by words — since the time of Moses the word had been acknowledged as being divine.

Even when it came to crossing the street, Macabéa was already a new person. A person enriched with a future. She felt within a hope more fierce than any anguish she had ever known. If she was no longer herself, this signified a loss that counted as a gain. Just as there was sentence of death, the fortune-teller had decreed sentence of life. Everything suddenly became so abundant and overwhelming, Macabéa felt like weeping. But she didn't weep: her eyes glistened like the setting sun.

The moment she stepped off the pavement, Destiny (bang) swift and greedy, whispered: now, quickly, for my hour has come!

And a yellow Mercedes, as huge as an ocean liner, knocked her down. At that very moment, in some remote corner of the world, a horse reared and gave a loud neigh, as if in response.

As she fell to the ground, Macabéa saw in time, before the car sped away, that Madame Carlota's prophecies were starting to come true. The yellow Mercedes was truly luxurious. Her fall was nothing serious, she thought to herself, she had simply lost her balance. Her head had struck the edge of the pavement and she remained lying there, her eyes turned towards the gutter. The trickle of blood coming from the wound on her temple was surprisingly thick and red. What I wanted to say was that despite everything, she belonged to a resistant and stubborn race of dwarfs that would one day vindicate the right to protest.

(I could turn the clock back and happily start again at the point when Macabéa was standing on the pavement — but it isn't for me to say whether the fair-haired foreigner looked at her. The fact is that I've already gone too far and there is no turning back. Just as well that I did not, nor do I intend to speak of death. I will simply call it an accident.)

Macabéa lay helpless by the side of the road. She felt drained of all emotion as she looked at the stones around the sewer and sprouting blades of wild grass; their greenness conveyed the most tender hope. Today, she thought, today is the dawn of my existence: I am born.

(Truth is always some inexplicable inner contact. Truth is unrecognizable. Therefore, doesn't it exist? No, for men it doesn't exist.)

Returning to the grass. For a creature as meagre as Macabéa, abundant nature was offering itself in a few sparse blades of grass growing in the gutter — were she to be offered the mighty ocean or lofty mountain peaks, her soul, even more chaste than her body, would hallucinate and her organism would explode, arms and intestines scattered here and there, a round, hollow head rolling at her feet — like a dismantled wax dummy.

Suddenly, Macabéa paid a little attention to herself. Could this be some muted earthquake? The land of Alagoas had opened in gaping cracks. She stared, just for the sake of staring, at the blades of grass. Grass in the great Metropolis of Rio de Janeiro. Adrift. Who knows if Macabéa had ever felt at some time that she, too, was adrift in the great unconquerable city? For her, Destiny had decreed a dark cul-de-sac and a street gutter. Was she suffering? I believe she was. Like a hen with its neck half-severed, running about in a panic and dripping blood. Except that the hen escapes — as one flees from pain — clucking in desperation. Macabéa struggled in silence.

I shall do everything possible to see that she doesn't die. But I feel such an urge to put her to sleep and then go off to sleep myself.

There was a gentle drizzle. Olímpico was right: all Macabéa was good for was for making sure that it rained. The fine drops of freezing rain gradually soaked into her clothes, making her feel extremely uncomfortable.

I ask myself: is every story that has ever been written in

this world, a story of suffering and affliction?

Some people appeared from nowhere in the cul-de-sac and gathered round Macabéa. They just stood there doing nothing just as people had always done nothing to help her; except that these people peered at her and this gave her an existence.

(But who am I to censure the guilty? The worst part is that I must forgive them. It is essential to arrive at an absolute zero so that we indifferently come to love or not to love the criminal who kills us. But I am no longer sure of myself: I must ask, without knowing whom I should ask, if it is really necessary to love the man who slays me; to ask who among you is slaying me. My life, stronger than myself, replies that it wants revenge at all costs. It warns me that I must struggle like someone drowning, even if I should perish in the end. If it be so, so be it.)

Is Macabéa about to die? How can I tell? Not even those onlookers could tell. Although someone from a nearby house, suspecting that she might be dying, placed a lit candle beside her body. The luxury of that generous flame appeared to sing of glory.

(I give the bare essentials, enhancing them with pomp, jewels and splendour. Is this how one should write? No, not by accretion but rather by denudation. But I am frightened of nakedness, for that is the final word.)

Meanwhile, Macabéa, lying on the ground, seemed to become more and more transformed into a Macabéa, as if she were arriving at herself.

Is this a melodrama? What I can say is that melodrama was the summit of her life. All lives are an art, and hers inclined towards an outburst of restless weeping with thunder and lightning.

A scrawny fellow appeared on the street-corner, wearing a threadbare jacket and playing the fiddle. I should explain that, when I was a child and living in Recife, I once saw this man as dusk was falling. The shrill, prolonged sound of his playing underlined in gold the mystery of that darkened street. On the ground, beside this pitiful fellow, there was a tin can which received the rattling coins of grateful by-standers as he played the dirge of their lives. It is only now that I have come to understand. Only now has the secret meaning dawned on me: the fiddler's music is an omen. I know that when I die, I shall hear him playing and that I shall crave for music, music, music.

Macabéa, Hail Mary, full of grace, serene land of promise, land of forgiveness, the time must come, *ora pro nobis*. I use myself as a form of knowledge. I know you through and through, by means of an incantation that comes from me to you. To stretch out savagely while an inflexible geometry vibrates behind everything. Macabéa remembered the docks. The docks went to the heart of her existence.

Macabéa ask for pardon? One must always ask. Why? Reply: it is so because it is so. Was it always so? It will always be so. And if it were not so? But I am saying that it is so. Very well.

It was quite obvious that Macabéa was still alive, for her enormous eyes went on blinking and her flat chest heaved and fell as she struggled for breath. But who can tell if she was not in need of dying? For there are moments when one needs a taste of death without even realizing it. Personally, I substitute the act of death with one of its symbols. A symbol that can be summarized by a deep kiss, not up against a wall, but mouth to mouth in the agony of pleasure that is death.

To my great joy, I find that the hour has not come for the film-star Macabéa to die. At least, I cannot divine if she gets her fair-haired foreigner. Pray for her and interrupt what-ever you're doing in order to breathe a little life into her, for Macabéa is presently adrift, like a door swinging in a never-ending breeze. I could resolve this story by taking the easy way out and murdering the infant child, but what I want is something more: I want life. Let my readers take a punch in the stomach to see how they enjoy it. For life is a punch in the stomach.

Meantime, Macabéa was nothing but a vague sentiment lying on the dirty paving stones. I could leave her lying there and simply not finish the story. But no. I shall go on until I reach that point where the atmosphere finishes, where the howling gale explodes, where the void makes a curve, where my breath takes me. Does my breath deliver me to God? I am so pure that I know nothing. I know only one thing: there is no need to pity God. Or perhaps there is?

Macabéa had enough life left in her to stir gently and take up the foetal position. She looked as grotesque as ever. Reluctant to surrender, yet avid for the great embrace. She embraced herself, longing for sweet nothingness. She was damned and didn't know it. She clung to a thread of consciousness and mentally repeated over and over again: I am, I am, I am. Precisely who she was, she was unable to say. She had searched in the deep, black essence of her own being, for that breath of life granted by God.

As she lay there, she felt the warmth of supreme happiness, for she had been born for death's embrace. Death is my favourite character in this story. Was Macabéa about to bid herself goodbye? I don't believe that she is going to die, for she has so much will to live. There was even a suggestion of sensuality in the way she lay there huddled up. Or is this because pre-death resembles some intense sensual longing? Macabéa's expression betrayed a grimace of desire. Things are ever vesperal and if she is not dying now, then like us, she has reached the vigil of death. Forgive me for reminding you, for I find it difficult to forgive myself for this clairvoyance.

A sensation as pleasurable, tender, horrifying, chilling and penetrating as love. Could this be the grace you call God? Yes? Were she about to die, she would pass from being a virgin to being a woman. No, this wasn't death. Death is not what I want for this girl: a mere collision that

83

amounted to nothing serious. Her struggle to live resembled something that she had never experienced before, virgin that she was, yet had grasped by intuition. For only now did she understand that a woman is born a woman from that first wail at birth. A woman's destiny is to be a woman. Macabéa had perceived the almost painful and vertiginous moment of overwhelming love. A painful and difficult reflowering that she enacted with her body and that other thing you call a soul and I call — what?

At that instant, Macabéa came out with a phrase that no one among the onlookers could understand. She said in a clear, distinct voice:

— As for the future.

Did she crave a future? I hear the ancient music of words upon words. Yes, it is so. At this very moment Macabéa felt nausea well up in the pit of her stomach and almost vomited. She felt like vomiting something that was not matter but luminous. Star with a thousand pointed rays.

What do I see now, that is so terrifying? I see that she has vomited a little blood, a great spasm, essence finally touching essence: victory!

And then — then suddenly the anguished cry of a seagull, suddenly the voracious eagle soaring on high with the tender lamb in its beak, the sleek cat mangling vermin, life devouring life.

Et tu, Brute?

Yes, this was the way I had hoped to announce that — that Macabéa was dead. The Prince of Darkness had triumphed. Coronation at last.

What was the truth about my Maca? It is enough to discover the truth that she no longer exists: the moment has passed. I ask myself: what is she? Reply: she is not.

But don't grieve for the dead: they know what they're doing. I have been to the land of the dead and after the most gruesome horrors I have come back redeemed. I am innocent! Do not devour me! I am not negotiable!

Alas, all is lost, and the greatest guilt would appear to be mine. Let them bathe my hands and feet and then — then let them anoint them with the holy, perfumed oils. Ah, such a longing for happiness. I try forcing myself to burst out laughing. But somehow I cannot laugh. Death is an encounter with self. Laid out and dead, Macabéa looked as imposing as a dead stallion. The best thing is still the following: not to die, for to die is not enough. It fails to achieve my greatest need: self-fulfilment.

Macabéa has murdered me.

She is finally free of herself and of me. Do not be frightened. Death is instantaneous and passes in a flash. I know, for I have just died with the girl. Forgive my dying. It was unavoidable. If you have kissed the wall, you can accept anything. But suddenly I make one last gesture of rebellion and start to howl: the slaughter of doves! To live is a luxury.

Suddenly it's all over.

Macabéa is dead. The bells were ringing without making any sound. I now understand this story. She is the imminence in those bells, pealing so softly.

The greatness of every human being.

Silence.

Should God descend on earth one day there would be a great silence.

The silence is such, that thought no longer thinks.

Was the ending of my story as grand as you expected? Dying, Macabéa became air. Vigorous air? I cannot say. She died instantaneously. An instant is that particle of time in which the tyre of a car going at full speed touches the ground, touches it no longer, then touches it again. Etc., etc., etc. At heart, Macabéa was little better than a music box sadly out of tune.

I ask you:

— What is the weight of light?

And now — now it only remains for me to light a cigarette and go home. Dear God, only now am I remembering that people die. Does that include me?

Don't forget, in the meantime, that this is the season for strawberries. Yes.

Acknowledgements

I SHOULD like to express my gratitude to Michael Schmidt, Robyn Marsack and the staff of Carcanet Press; also to the following colleagues and friends who offered useful advice and criticism: Paul Berman, Eudinyr Fraga, Patricia Bins, Carlos Sachs, Teresa Nunes, Amelia Hutchinson and Arnold Hinchliffe; and finally to Stefanie Goodfellow for valuable material assistance, and to Nancy Stålhammer, who typed the manuscript with scrupulous care.

Giovanni Pontiero
Manchester, June 1985

Afterword

CLARICE Lispector died of cancer at the age of fifty-six on 9 December 1977. *The Hour of the Star* was published that same year and acclaimed by the critics as 'a regional allegory' of extraordinary awareness and insight. The tale of Macabéa, however, can be read at different levels and lends itself to various interpretations. The book's subtle interplay of fiction and philosophy sums up Clarice Lispector's unique talent as a writer and her lasting influence on contemporary Brazilian writing.

Shortly before she became seriously ill, Clarice Lispector began to experience an almost obsessive nostalgia for Recife in the North-eastern State of Pernambuco, where she had spent her childhood. This nostalgia resulted in a sentimental journey to renew contact with scenes and locations associated with her earliest perceptions. Back in Rio, she also began to make regular trips to the street market specializing in crafts and wares from North-eastern Brazil, that takes place every Sunday in the São Cristóvão district of the city. It was here that the author could observe at her leisure the lowly immigrants from the North-east who came to buy and sell or simply to watch, re-enacting for a day the customs and traditions of their native region. The São Cristóvão market evoked the sights and sounds Clarice Lispector had savoured as a child and the unmistakable physical traits of the North-easterners who gathered there provided her with mental sketches for the principal characters in *The Hour of the Star*.

The nucleus of the narrative centres on the misfortunes of Macabéa, a humble girl from a region plagued by drought and poverty, whose future is determined by her inexperience, her ugliness and her total anonymity. Macabéa's speech and dress betray her origins. An orphaned child from the backwoods of Alagoas, who was brought up by a forbidding aunt in Maceió before making her way to the slums of Acre Street in the heart of Rio de Janeiro's red-light district. Gauche and rachitic, Macabéa has poverty and ill-health written all over her: a creature conditioned from birth and already singled out as one of the world's inevitable losers.

Her humdrum existence can be summarized in few words: Macabéa is an appallingly bad typist, she is a virgin, and her favourite drink is Coca-Cola. She is the perfect foil for a bullying employer, a philandering boy friend, and her workmate Glória, who has all the attributes Macabéa sadly lacks.

Macabéa's abrupt exit under the front wheels of a yellow Mercedes is as absurd and inevitable as all the other disasters that befall this hopeless misfit.

The grim social factors governing her bleak existence are

all too familiar in the lower strata of Brazilian society. Factually summarized, Macabéa's history suggests a stereotype from a sociological survey. But the magic begins when Clarice Lispector starts to investigate the psychological consequences of poverty. The compounded effects of ignorance, fear, and privation result in perverse twists of fortune. Yet behind this unpromising façade there remain traces of resilience and the will to survive. Macabéa's faltering moments of self-recognition are registered by a series of explosions — both psychological and emotional. There is nothing forced or deliberate in Macabéa's aimless progress through life. Physically and emotionally stunted, this antiheroine holds her breath and waits for destiny to do its worst. The girl's puzzled response to her alien surroundings reveals unexpected strengths: the brash metropolis and its pressures fail to diminish her will to live. Deprived of any material expectations, Macabéa makes a virtue of her emptiness by settling for the vagaries of faith. Judged objectively, faith in her situation seems unjustified and even perverse. Viewed subjectively, however, faith bestows a singular state of grace.

Macabéa's inner being is jolted by momentary perceptions — by sudden discoveries that outweigh her understanding and leave her perplexed and disorientated. First there is the shattering awareness of her own body, a discovery that aptly coincides with May — the month of love and nuptials. Then comes a short-lived romance followed by betrayal and rejection.

As Macabéa stumbles from one embarrassing exposure to another, one can virtually hear the author muse: 'there but for the grace of God go I'. This diary of a nobody gains in strength and meaning as a game of counter-reflections develops between the author and her protagonist. For, while it is true that Lispector would have us believe in a male narrator, she does not relinquish involvement. The advantage she claims to derive from this masculine alias is one of emotional detachment. Its validity and necessity, however, is debatable.

As in all her previous narratives, Clarice Lispector narrates *from within*. In *The Hour of the Star* her own unmistakable presence often merges with that of Macabéa. From the outset, she draws an interesting comparison between herself as the writer and the character she is creating, between reason and instinct, between knowledge and innocence, between the powers of imagination and unadorned reality. The creative writer is able to transform reality. Hence Clarice Lispector's compassionate attitude towards her unresourceful heroine 'who did not know how to adorn reality'. Macabéa is puzzled and frustrated by the enormity of the external world, but she enjoys one considerable privilege: inner freedom.

The Hour of the Star is comparable with Clarice Lispector's earlier work insofar as the central character provides a nucleus for a wider exploration of existential problems. Basic assumptions about human responses to truth, happiness, and integrity are challenged and reassessed. The traumas of the women — adolescent, mature, innocent, and experienced — that dominated the stories of *Family Ties* are resurrected in *The Hour of the Star*. Here, too, we find the same lucid perceptions about the perils of human existence: the same relentless thirst for 'spiritual catharsis'. Macabéa's 'inviolable secret' reflects the drama of every sentient creature. The frequent references to God and the supernatural attest to the mystical dimension here as in most of Clarice Lispector's narratives. Her Jewish-Slavonic ancestry is important in this context. A bond has crystallized between the presence of a divine spirit exacting justice and the creative process itself. Salvation ultimately comes in the form of self-discovery and authentic self-expression.

The aphorisms woven into the text are beguiling, and more beguiling still is the manner in which the author works from a reduction and even an absence of anything concrete. Her dazzling insights are extracted from the most opaque abstractions, above all the human mind when clouded by emotions. The rare moment of ecstasy is sparked off by the most fragile aspect of every living creature, namely his aspirations. Apparent contradictions in Macabéa's faulty reasoning are somehow made to sound convincing. The mental gyrations unfailingly spiral from a principle of order: 'before the prehistory there was the prehistory of the prehistory and there was the *never* and the *yes*'; philosophical probings that remain beyond the reach of Macabéa's understanding yet, in her own spontaneous way, she perceives their significance. Macabéa's tragic question: 'Who am I?' unwittingly echoes the major preoccupation of every mortal. No less tragic or familiar is the question that follows on: 'Am I monster or is this what it means to be a person?' When the author intervenes in the narrative to remind the reader that 'he who probes is incomplete', she is simply reaffirming our spiritual and emotional fragmentation. The human being who fails to question his or her mortal state is merely vegetating and never likely to transgress his own limitations. Lacking her creator's intellectual powers, Macabéa moves to much the same conlcusions by purely intuitive means. Instinctive desires and aspirations draw her into the same rich labyrinth of unresolved enigmas.

Both writer and character know that existence can appear to be both absurd and illogical, yet ironically it is the simple-witted Macabéa who seems better equipped to cope with life's reversals. While Clarice Lispector battles with concepts, Macabéa tries to penetrate a web of superstitions and fantasies. Macabéa's fears are instinctive and irrational. Clarice Lispector's apprehensions are the fruit of scrupulous introspection. Yet the roots of this spiritual crisis are basically the same. Their tragic perceptions of life are ultimately indistinguishable. Both writer and character find themselves on the margin of society, for both of them respond to an inner law that means nothing to the world.

Macabéa's two attempts to be positive are significant. First, her visit to a third-rate doctor in the hope of healing her body. Second, her visit to the clairvoyante Madame Carlota, in the hope of healing her soul. These constitute two of the wittiest and most moving episodes Lispector ever wrote. The doctor, who has lost any sense of vocation after a lifetime of treating impoverished patients, dreams of getting rich so that he can do exactly as he pleases: *nothing*. The confrontation between the ingenuous Macabéa and the cynical practitioner is strangely revealing.

Macabéa's ineffectual attempts to explain her needs only provoke hostility and misunderstanding: her seemingly passive acceptance of disaster and misfortune arouse puzzlement and exasperation. She seems incapable of meeting the real world on its own terms. The society in which she finds herself has little use for 'the pure happiness of idiots'. Hence the gulf between Macabéa and her rival Glória, who has all the right credentials for material success; between Macabéa and her worthless boyfriend Olímpico; between Macabéa and the absurd Madame Carlota, who has more faces than Janus (clairvoyante/fan of Jesus/prostitute/brothel keeper). Macabéa's goal is much more modest yet at the same time much more difficult to achieve, namely, to establish her own identity. Macabéa's heroism consists in not being heroic. Her struggle has been notable for its reticence. A lifetime of anonymity decreed and endured.

The closing reflections on death carry a poignant note. Macabéa's premonitions are shared by Lispector. What Macabéa perceives, Lispector has always known, namely that: 'Death is an encounter with self'. A brief, ecstatic moment of transition as corporeal form is miraculously transformed into 'vigorous air'. The promise of sudden release is inviting, but life demands the greater courage. The *carpe diem* sentiments of the book's closing sentence remind us that Lispector's heroines never withdraw from the struggle until summoned. One proves oneself in life rather than in death.

The Hour of the Star is not Clarice Lispector's first serious attempt to clarify her approach to the craft of fiction. Many of the concepts expressed here have been voiced before in works like *The Foreign Legion* and *Family Ties*. There is, nevertheless, a bolder attempt in this last book to analyse in greater detail the mysterious nature of inspiration and the elusive process of growth and enhancement. In *The Hour of the Star*, Clarice Lispector is intent upon linking the structure of the narrative with a subtle exploration of the creative process as seen by the artist.

The metaphors the author derives from parable, legend, and anecdote are effective because they are used sparingly and ingeniously slanted. The author prefers sparseness to accumulation, just as she finds prophecy infinitely more suggestive than the definition. As in all her writing, the dimension of mystery is sacrosanct. Mystical forces are ever present. There is always a note of divination, however serious or humorous, however formal or colloquial the prose. Things intimate and remote frequently overlap. Her asides to the reader, as distractions, uncertainties, and obstacles interrupt the creative process, underline the attendant problems as the writer struggles for direction and clarification. They also show how a writer may question the validity of the characters in a narrative even after those characters have assumed an independent existence. On occasion, their development may even run at a tangent to the author's original intentions. For, once the creative process is under way, new forces mysteriously exert their influence. The author sometimes tries to retreat, only to discover that it is much too late. The writer may grow tired of the characters to whom she has given birth, but they resist dismissal.

Meditation has always outweighed mere description in Clarice Lispector's writing. Characters and situations are rapidly sketched in with a few bare essentials. The characterization of Macabéa is centred on the girl's delicate and

95

vague existence. Doubt outweighs certainty in the author's analysis of the human psyche. Even the aphorisms in the book invite discussion rather than bland approval. The cliché is reconstituted into some riveting new insight. The author reminds us of the hidden power of words. Macabéa's whole existence is changed by words capable of banishing her sterility: 'the fruit of the word' transforms her into a woman.

In the next breath Clarice Lispector defines *The Hour of the Star* as a book 'made without words . . . a mute photograph . . . a silence . . . a question'. For in all her narratives she treats silence like sorrow, and transforms it into a fount of eternal truths.

Giovanni Pontiero